Seminary Development News
The First Ten Years

Edited by
David L. Heetland

Supported by a grant from
Lilly Endowment Inc.
Indianapolis, Indiana

Library of Congress Catalog Card Number: 96-94829
Heetland, David
  Seminary Development News: The First Ten Years.
ISBN 0-9654902-0-3

Contents

Preface

In the mid-1980s, John Zehring, then vice president for development at Bangor Theological Seminary in Bangor, Maine, had a dream for a newsletter for seminary development officers. He shared his dream with ATS's Development and Institutional Advancement Program (DIAP) committee, and they recommended that a special newsletter be established for a three-year experimental period. The newsletter was to serve the following purposes:

1. provide information regarding financial development programs, trends, and state of the art issues;

2. interpret current financial development trends according to the issues and needs of theological schools and their development staffs;

3. strengthen the identity of seminary development officers by focusing on their roles in theological education and enhancing their professional competence and careers;

4. nurture a stronger sense of collegiality and shared interests of development personnel;

5. serve as a means of emphasizing and strengthening the capacity of theological schools to attract financial resources that are essential to their well-being;

6. determine the long-term communication and information needs of seminary development personnel.

In 1987 a grant proposal was submitted to the Lilly Endowment requesting funding for a quarterly newsletter for three years. The request was granted, John Zehring was named editor, and in the winter of 1987 the first issue of *Seminary Development News* was published.

The newsletter was distributed on a complimentary basis to all seminary presidents, development personnel, trustee development committee chairpersons, and foundation heads, and was immediately well-received.

Through careful stewardship the three-year grant lasted

nearly four years. John Zehring resigned as editor at the end of 1990 to assume a new position outside of theological education. I assumed the editorship in 1991 and continue to serve as editor today.

A second Lilly Endowment grant was received to enable publication of *Seminary Development News* for an additional three years (1991-92 through 1993-94). Careful stewardship of this grant permitted publication for five years (through 1995-96), and some money earmarked for *Seminary Development News* in another Lilly Endowment grant to ATS will allow publication through the 1996-97 academic year.

Seminary Development News has moved well beyond its initial three-year experiment, and has become an important communication piece for development officers, CEOs, and trustees of theological seminaries in the United States and Canada.

Two readership surveys (one in the summer of 1989 and another in the summer of 1993) attest to the newsletter's usefulness. The surveys found that ninety-one percent find it helpful or very helpful, eighty-four percent read all or most of it, seventy-two percent share it with someone else, and sixty-eight percent file it for future reference. According to the surveys, *Seminary Development News* ranks highest of all DIAP-sponsored programs, surpassing seminars, research, and special projects.

The newsletter has met and exceeded its original purposes, and has helped to build a stronger sense of collegiality and professionalism among development officers in theological education. Since its inception 120 authors have been featured on the pages of the newsletter.

In anticipation of the tenth anniversary of *Seminary Development News,* the editorial board proposed the publication of a book of some of the timely articles from the first ten years. They believed that a book would accomplish several purposes:

1. serve as an orientation manual for new persons entering theological education development work;

2. serve as an alternative resource for those requesting back issues, which are rapidly being depleted;

3. serve as a development reference book for all seminary libraries;

4. serve as a fitting tribute to the first ten years of *Seminary Development News.*

The Lilly Endowment recognized the value of such a book and graciously agreed to underwrite the cost of publishing it. The book will be made available to attendees at DIAP Seminar '97. Additional copies will be sent to all ATS seminaries, and a number of copies will be reserved for orientation manuals and for future requests.

All of the articles in the book originally appeared in *Seminary Development News.* The book's introduction by Fred Hofheinz was a major presentation at the 1992 DIAP Seminar, the tenth anniversary of that organization.

Seminary Development News could not have achieved the success it has without the generous financial support from the Lilly Endowment. Special thanks to Fred Hofheinz, program director for religion at Lilly, for his vision and unwavering commitment to strengthen the development enterprise in theological education. His support of the DIAP organization, *Seminary Development News,* and this book is deeply appreciated.

Thanks also to those persons who faithfully served on the *Seminary Development News* editorial board in the past (John Zehring, David Harkins, Mollie Fenger, John Gilbert, Jr., Diane Spence, and Daniel Conway) and to those who provide outstanding leadership on the current editorial board (Richard Eppinga, Michaeline O'Dwyer, and Kate Welles-Snyder).

Finally, heartfelt thanks to the many contributors to *Seminary Development News.* Although it was not possible to include every article in this book, all of you have made an important contribution to development in theological education by sharing so willingly your wisdom and insights. May the newsletter and this book continue to nurture a strong sense of collegiality and shared vision among us.

David Heetland

Introduction

Celebrating Ten Years of
Development in Theological Education

Fred Hofheinz

I am deeply honored to be with you as you celebrate this
tenth anniversary gathering of seminary development officers. I
was present at the first of these gatherings in St. Louis a decade
ago, and at several of the seminars in subsequent years. Since I
had a bit to do with the conception, gestation, and birth of this
idea, I have watched its growth to maturity with quite a bit of
interest.

I joined the staff of the Lilly Endowment in May of 1973
and so have had a long and interesting career as an institutional
bird watcher of seminaries.

Although the Lilly Endowment had been supporting theological schools in various ways from its founding in 1937, I
would date its first formal program interest with seminaries ecu-
menically and nationally from 1975, for it was in that year that
the Endowment, as a newly emerging national foundation, gave
approval to launch a broad-based comprehensive program of support for theological education across the United States and
Canada. All that the Endowment has done with and for theological schools since that time comes from that decision by the
Endowment board.

In our staff report to our Board, the Religion Division
staff described certain elements that we deemed necessary ingredients for any comprehensive strategy for grants in this field.
Many of those ingredients still mark the strategies of our grantmaking to this day. For example, we are gathered here today
under the aegis of the Association of Theological Schools under
a grant from the Endowment. That is consonant with our ordinary
method of making grants to the ATS in order to serve the entire

seminary enterprise. Another element of our grantmaking strategy at that time, and one we still use, is to concentrate the majority of our grantmaking for individual schools within a competitive grant framework. In our 1975 Board memorandum, the staff proposed "a series of competitive grants programs designed to strengthen the work of seminaries at crucial points." The Board gave the go-ahead to proceed in this fashion, and we on the staff then began to cast around for promising themes upon which to base competitive grants programs.

We consulted with a wide variety of persons within and without seminaries to try to determine the most promising emerging issues in theological education upon which we ought to center our new competitive grants offerings. A variety of themes surfaced in these conversations, most of them having to do with perceived needs of seminary administrators and faculty for Lilly support of various ongoing or emerging educational programs. One very loud and persuasive voice suggested that we give serious consideration to an issue which he was convinced might be the defining challenge for theological schools over the next decade. That persuasive voice belonged to Warren H. Deem, a Presbyterian layman, management consultant, and entrepreneur who was the first lay member of the executive committee of the ATS.

Bob Lynn and I, who were the two people at the Endowment staffing this new Lilly enterprise, were both a bit skeptical when Warren tried to persuade us of the importance of concentrating one of our competitive programs on helping seminaries begin to develop the kinds of resources which, Deem was convinced, would be necessary to help seminaries survive the rough decade which lay ahead. But Warren was so persuasive that we agreed to risk one of the five competitive programs for which we had funding on this wild idea, and with Warren's help we prepared materials for a Competitive Grants Program entitled "Creation of Strategies for Development." Bob Lynn was so convinced that this program would be uninteresting to schools that it was the only one of the five programs offered that year which he turned over completely to me, his junior colleague. Well, Deem of course was right and the rest is history.

Fifty-two seminaries submitted development proposals in that 1975 competition, by far the single largest number of applications in any of our five competitive programs. As I look back upon those proposals from the vantage point of 1992, I am overwhelmed by their simplicity and lack of sophistication. Yet taken together they told remarkable stories about the state of the financing of theological education in the middle of the 1970s. Proposal after proposal said very much the same thing: This seminary has for years depended on the denominations and the churches to keep it going. That funding is now rapidly drying up and we know we must find some way to discover and cultivate new donors because if we don't we won't last the next five years. We think there are people out there who might be persuaded to help us, but we have neither a plan, nor the personnel, to get this job done. If Lilly will only give us the money to hire a person to become our fund raiser and provide some money to equip an office for this person, we'll go right to work.

That is, of course, a caricature, but not very much of one. Though there are no adequate records about this, I would venture that in 1975 fewer than one-third of ATS seminaries had anything resembling a professional development office, and those that did were, for the most part, staffed by retired ministers or former insurance salesmen who, though well intentioned, had no training or understanding of the development function. Nonetheless, it was clear that Lilly had struck a real live vein and that there was a powerful need for more work in this arena. Indeed, helping seminaries in development became Lilly's most lasting work from the 1970s.

In 1975 the Endowment offered five competitive programs, of which development was only one. In 1976 development was one of three such competitions. By 1977 this work had become so critical that the only Lilly seminary competition that year was for development.

By the time 1978 rolled around we had helped a signifi-

4

cant number of schools get their development efforts launched. It was now becoming clear that the most pervasive need within theological seminaries was for trained development professionals. The best ideas and the most promising plans of seminaries were severely handicapped by the absence of skilled development professionals. Several things were at work causing this problem. For the most part seminaries were unable or unwilling to compete in the open market for experienced people. Seminaries were forced, therefore, to turn either to very inexperienced folks (and for those there were few if any training opportunities) or to attempt to hire folks with a bit of experience who, as soon as they got better, were lured away from seminaries into higher paying jobs. It became clear to us that the next phase of our work had to address this situation.

Beginning in 1978, and for the next several years, we operated a mini-school for development officers. By the time the last of our training seminars for beginning development officers ended in 1981 the Endowment had trained more than sixty development professionals at an equal number of schools and had, I believe, achieved a certain kind of "critical mass" of professionals in the universe of theological schools.

Having helped raise the consciousness of the seminary community about the importance and promise of development through our competitive grants of 1975, '76, and '77, and having trained a substantial corps of development professionals from 1978 through 1981, it was now time for the Lilly Endowment to move on to other issues. But before doing that it was essential that we design and promote one final chapter in our support for seminary development. In the spring of 1982 I sought to convince an initially reluctant ATS staff that they ought to submit a proposal to the Endowment to support a program of ongoing attention to the development concerns of theological seminaries. This effort, which became the DIAP program, was first supported by a $300,000 grant awarded in June of 1982 and has continued with decreasing Lilly support ever since.

Let me make an observation about the decade which preceded the establishment of this DIAP effort, a decade which I believe was the most important in the long history of the financing of theological education. When Warren Deem first came to the Endowment to convince us to get involved in this work, he did so because he had been observing a disturbing trend. Largely because of Deem's influence, the ATS began collecting financial information from seminaries in the 1968-69 school year. In that year the total enterprise of theological education ran a collective $1.7 million deficit, and the situation was getting increasingly worse. In fact, beginning in 1968 there were seven consecutive deficit years. The situation then began to turn around, largely because of the heightened interest in development by theological school leaders. The decade between the 1970-71 academic year and the 1981-82 academic year was the most dramatic. In 1971 total expenditures at all ATS schools were $118 million and there was a total deficit of just over $5 million. A decade later, after the double digit inflation years of the late 1970s, the total expenditures for ATS schools had nearly tripled to more than $333 million. Nevertheless, that year ended with a total surplus of nearly $10 million. I don't believe there will ever be another such volatile decade in the history of higher education. By the providence of God seminaries got involved in development work not a moment too soon!

Fifteen years ago seminary development officers did not have an annual meeting. With a few notable exceptions, they did not exercise leadership roles in their institutions or influence the way in which seminaries were administered. Like many other church-related organizations, seminaries tended to regard fund raising as a necessary evil. They engaged in fund raising activities reluctantly when there was an urgent need, but even though the needs were genuine, they often raised money apologetically, sometimes promising not to ask again "if only you'll give this one time." How far we have come in such a short time!

Many of you may know DIAP only through this series of annual seminars. In addition to this ongoing training function, DIAP has also identified two long-range objectives which are

6

more subtle, but which I believe are even more ambitious.

    1. To promote an understanding of development as both a ministry and an expression of organizational stewardship. It has been my observation over the past decade or so that seminaries have had to develop a radically different approach to the way the theology and practice of stewardship are understood and experienced in the administration of the seminary. This new approach is characterized by a more proactive and collaborative exercise of leadership on the part of seminary officials and by a greater willingness to share the mission of theological education with others.

    Seminary leaders who once understood their stewardship responsibilities in a low-key, passive way have been challenged by the demands of the past decade and a half to be much more active in their stewardship. These challenges, whether of enrollment, finance, or church politics, have demonstrated that seminary boards can no longer afford to be merely the quiet guardians of a seminary's mission. Instead they must work with the president and faculty to shape a vision for the future and to develop the strategic plans that are needed to keep theological education academically, pastorally, and fiscally vibrant.

    In a very real way, the financial and fund raising crises of the past ten to fifteen years have helped seminaries see that good stewardship means much more than just the prudent management of a school's operating and endowment funds. It also means accepting responsibility for setting new directions and for developing new resources, which is what the development and institutional advancement of seminaries is all about.

    Good leadership is essential to successful development because the days are gone when people gave to church-related organizations merely out of a sense of obligation. Today, people give because they choose to give, and they choose to give to those organizations which can demonstrate that they 1) make a difference in our world, and 2) are fully accountable for the quality of their leadership and for their use of the human, physical, and financial resources entrusted to their care.

In today's economic climate, success in raising significant dollars requires the kind of leadership which can show that a church-related organization truly responds to the needs of the human family. Indeed, the ability of an organization's leaders to set new directions for the future and to inspire confidence in others is absolutely critical to the success of a contemporary development program.

In addition to good leadership, successful development programs require consistent, value-oriented communications. Because people no longer give primarily out of a sense of obligation, they much more readily ask questions: "Why should I give to the seminary? Doesn't the denomination which owns the seminary cover its costs? Where do my annual appeal dollars go? How are the seminary's endowment funds being managed? What real difference will my gifts make?"

These are legitimate questions which deserve to be answered. What is different today from just a generation ago is the serious way in which these questions are asked and the fact that people will not give, except in a token way, unless they are satisfied with the answers. In my experience, it is rare that a seminary deliberately refuses to answer these legitimate questions. Most often we find that the inability to communicate clearly why funds are needed and how they are used results from a lack of awareness about the importance of frequent, personal communication.

Most church-related organizations, and that includes seminaries, are not accustomed to doing the kind of sustained, value-oriented communication which is necessary to inform, motivate, and acknowledge the gifts of substance that are needed today. Occasional newsletters and fund raising brochures represent the standard repertoire of our limited public relations and marketing efforts. During a campaign we intensify our efforts somewhat, but once that is over we tend to revert to occasional, indirect communications.

Once again, it is important to note that people give because they choose to give, and they choose to give to those organizations which they think are making a difference and are fully accountable. Today, regardless of their loyalty to the church, even generous people will not make substantial gifts to a seminary unless their legitimate questions are answered in compelling and convincing ways. Indeed, when we challenge the local congregation, or the church community as a whole, to embrace the theology and practice of stewardship we are inviting them to become even more discriminating in their giving to church-related organizations.

2. *To encourage the full integration of development into the life of the seminary.* Over the years, with the help of Endowment funding, ATS has sponsored many seminars and training programs designed to help trustees, presidents, and deans in the exercise of their leadership and stewardship responsibilities. ATS has also successfully used its DIAP program to elevate the status of development and institutional advancement from the "necessary evil" it was ten to fifteen years ago to a much more significant role in the enterprise of theological education. Unfortunately, however, development is still not fully integrated into the life of many seminaries. This has unavoidable consequences not only for the school's fund raising efforts, but also for the kind of education which is being provided to the future leaders of our church.

From my rather unique perspective, I have been able to observe the various ways that seminaries and other church-related organizations have planned and implemented their development programs. Over the years I have observed many successes and many failures, and I have come to the conclusion that the most successful seminary development programs are the ones that are fully integrated into the school's mission and purpose.

It is sometimes said that the difference between stewardship and fund raising is that fund raising is based on an organization's needs, while stewardship is based on the principle of giving back to God a proportionate share of the blessings we have received. In my experience, good fund raising is rarely need-based. In fact, when fund raising is seen as part of a comprehensive development program, it is usually based on a sense of mission and values, not on a catalog of needs. And in the context of total development, successful fund raising is an expression of good stewardship, not an obstacle to it.

As you can imagine, during my eighteen plus years at Lilly Endowment I have read hundreds of grant proposals. The most compelling and convincing of these don't focus on institutional needs; they focus on the mission of the organization and on the spiritual principles which underlie the organization's religious or cultural heritage. In fact, when needs are referred to, it is almost always in the context of *human* needs (for programs and services that will make a difference in people's lives) and not on the needs of the operating budget.

I have also observed that, while it is important to have a written case statement which expresses an organization's mission and its plans for the future, the best case statements are communicated orally—from one person to another—by telling the organization's story in ways that encourage others to become partners in its mission.

The concept of partnership is what distinguishes a development program that is fully integrated from one that is merely tolerated as a "necessary evil." There are several telling signs which indicate that a seminary has a development program that is deeply rooted in its identity and mission as a theological school. These are among the most important:

when the board, administration, and faculty truly seek to build relationships among community leaders, alums, and friends that encourage participation in the seminary's mission and goals;

when the seminary's development office is regarded as an extension of the school's mission which communicates values and invites others to share in the ministry of theological education;

when donors are respected and appreciated as colleagues rather than as "wealthy people" or "movers and shakers" who must be tolerated because of their wealth and influence;

when the widow's mite is valued as highly as the gifts of

the largest donor, not only because of pious sentiment but also because gifts of substance are encouraged and welcomed from all donors.

In my experience, this kind of radical grounding of development in the mission and purpose of a theological school has profound implications for its understanding of where the development program fits in the life of the seminary. It also has very practical implications for the amount of money that is raised and for the amount of time that trustees, seminary presidents, and development officers devote to planning and implementing development programs.

During the past fifteen years, Lilly Endowment has sponsored a variety of development education programs for church-related organizations and other human service agencies. While each program has reflected the unique character and differences of the organizations involved, there have been some remarkable similarities. One of the most consistent themes in all of the development education programs we've funded is the essential role that the organization's leaders play in the total fund raising process. In fact, if I were asked to identify the single most important element in a successful development program, on the basis of Lilly Endowment's experience I would have to say that it is the personal involvement of leadership in the design and implementation of the overall fund raising plan.

Why is leadership so important to the success or failure of an organization's fund raising efforts? The answer can be found in the distinction that we made earlier between need-based fund raising and the effort to develop resources based on an organization's mission and its plans for the future.

Need-based fund raising does not require much in the way of creativity or vision or personal involvement. If the roof needs to be repaired, you fix it. If the old computer system is outdated, you replace it. But a true development program whose goal is growth-in-mission needs leadership and vision. It needs the firm direction and active participation of those who are responsible for carrying out the organization's mission and long-range goals. And it needs the strong endorsement of recognized community leaders who can testify to both the importance of the cause and the credibility of the organization.

Regardless of whether the organization is a seminary or any other church-related organization, more often than not the involvement of its leadership determines the success or failure of its long-term development efforts. That means that the leaders of church-related organizations must own and accept their essential role in the fund raising process. It also means that new emphasis needs to be placed on the critical role that volunteer leaders play in an organization's development program.

Today we are gradually beginning to see that good leadership and good stewardship both require that the leaders of church-related organizations (including bishops and pastors as well as seminary presidents and board members) participate actively in the effort to identify, cultivate, and solicit the gifts of time, talent, and treasure that are needed to carry out the mission of the church. Indeed, the days are gone when a seminary president or board could delegate the total responsibility for fund raising to a staff member or a group of dedicated volunteers.

Most church leaders, and I include seminary presidents in that group, are not wild about the increasing amount of time which they must spend raising money. But the seminaries which have been the most successful in development have learned that the investments of time, personnel, and money which they have made in this important aspect of their ministry are well worth it. A development program which is truly integrated into the life of the seminary is clearly focused on that organization's mission and goals. Its outreach to others builds relationships and generates support, so that the seminary's investments in its development program directly support its growth-in-mission.

Over the years research sponsored by the Endowment has helped seminary leaders to see that it is in their own best interests to make development and institutional advancement an integral part of their stewardship of the school's mission. The result is an increasing awareness that successful fund raising is the result of leadership styles that can encourage growth-in-mission through decisive leadership and a true spirit of collaboration with those individuals, foundations, and even corporations, which have a stake in the future of theological education.

The past decade and a half have shown seminaries in the United States and Canada that the future of theological education depends on their ability to develop new attitudes about stewardship and development. For the most part seminary leaders have taken this challenge to heart and have responded with a sense of dedication and commitment (if not enthusiasm) to the demands of development and institutional advancement. They have also learned, sometimes the hard way, that growth-in-mission requires forms of leadership and accountability that are relatively new to church-related organizations.

As I discern the growing signs of the times in the financing of American religion, I believe that the next two decades will expand this challenge beyond the confines of our seminary campuses to the entire universe of religious agencies. If the Stewardship and Development study co-sponsored by St. Meinrad and Christian Theological Seminary accurately reflects the negative attitudes of church leaders today concerning administration, finance, and fund raising, it will be very difficult for church leaders to adopt the radical new approaches to leadership, stewardship, and development that will be needed to promote the growth-in-mission of tomorrow's church.

With this in mind, it is more important than ever for seminaries to lead the way in stewardship and development. Indeed, I believe that the head start that theological schools have gotten in the last fifteen years makes it imperative for seminaries to start to preach what they have been practicing; namely, that good stewardship requires vision, decisive leadership, and a willingness to invite others to invest their time, talent, and treasure in the mission of the church. If I am right about this, then seminaries have both a tremendous opportunity and a tremendous leadership responsibility ahead of them.

If organized religion is to continue to play its rightful

role in the fabric of American society, church leaders must learn in the seminary (as well as in the field) how to be good stewards of the human, physical, and financial resources of the church. They must come to see development not as a necessary evil, but as a very practical and profound expression of the personal and organizational stewardship which all of us are called to exercise out of gratitude to God for the many gifts which each of us has received.

Chapter One:
Theology and Fund Raising

The Ministry of Institutional Advancement

Harold R. Blatt

I had my heart set on being a missionary. My experience in the Pacific at the end of World War II confirmed my calling to "preach the gospel" in a foreign land.

How disappointing then to apply for missionary work and be asked to accept an assignment to the Philippines as director of stewardship. My immediate response was no thanks. I preferred to be a "real" missionary.

Eventually I did accept the stewardship appointment. Two things happened. First, it set the course of my career. Second, I discovered a ministry that has been fully rewarding and continues to confirm my original call as a minister of Jesus Christ.

My experience in the Philippines, a third-world nation, was particularly helpful in sharpening my understanding of stewardship as a viable ministry. A people "too poor to give" learned Paul's secret of "gracious giving." The success of our stewardship program had a profound effect on the vitality of the church and its mission.

Whether the institution helped is a church, denomination, or educational institution, the reward to the fund raiser is the same: to have had a major role in helping advance the kingdom of God.

Colleagues who enter advancement work from the pastorate may sometimes fear they will lose the joy of ministering to the personal needs of individuals. After all, more than one minister who has entered advancement work has been asked, "Why are you leaving the ministry?" Ministering to institutions is a different ball game from ministering to individuals. Fund raising is still a "people" business and good stewardship is strongly related to "spiritual development." Yet, a ministry to institutions requires us to reconceptualize our role as ministers.

We who represent theological schools have a distinct advantage. Being even indirectly involved in the preparation of men and women for ministry gives a stronger sense of fulfillment than might be true anywhere else. Many theological schools today would simply cease to be in business without our efforts. Certainly all of them would find their academic and scholarship programs seriously curtailed.

In the apostle Paul's teachings on giving in II Corinthians 8 & 9, he refers to the collection of funds as a "gracious work" and a "ministry."

Paul makes it clear that the experience of giving is a two-way street. It not only helps the cause, but it also has a spiritual effect on the donor and all others who observe it. In Paul's words, "the ministry of this service is not only fully supplying the needs of the saints, but is also overflowing through many thanksgivings to God" (II Corinthians 9:12 ASV).

It is this spiritual dimension of fund raising that brings the greatest joy. Reaching an annual or campaign goal brings a sense of pleasure, if not relief. But seeing lives change through a deepening understanding and practice of stewardship makes all the effort worthwhile.

Paul's insight provides a rationale for all the myriad tasks involved in "advancement." Public relations, publications, special events—all these activities are equally important and worthy of being considered ministry. A recognition event for one donor or many is all part of the "gracious work."

In any task it is easy to get bogged down in details, and yet, a staff person with a gift for details is a godsend. It is not always easy working behind the scenes, making sure that a special event is running smoothly, and likely getting no public credit for a job well done.

For me, the history and reputation of the institution where I work has a salutary effect on my morale. The feeling that there is a "great cloud of witnesses"—alums, faculty, trustees,

17

and donors, all past and present—gives great encouragement even when one is tired and lonely and miles away from home. At such times, I may even find myself saying, "How lucky I am to be involved in this kind of work."

In seminary advancement, our lives have been immeasurably enriched by our chosen profession. We pause now and then as we see God at work in our area of ministry and say with the great apostle, "Thanks be to God for God's indescribable gift."

Stewardship and Development:
A Theological Perspective

Daniel Conway

I am fortunate to have spent the past year and a half directing a research project called the Stewardship and Development Study. With the help of funding from Lilly Endowment, St. Meinrad School of Theology and Christian Theological Seminary co-sponsored this study as a way of "helping churches prepare their leaders to be good stewards of their churches' human, physical, and financial resources."

The Stewardship and Development Study had several objectives:

1. to identify the programs that are currently offered by seminaries in the United States and Canada in the areas of leadership, stewardship, and management;

2. to discover what seminary presidents, deans, and faculty think about the importance of these subject areas;

3. to survey pastors' attitudes about their administrative responsibilities and about the programs which seminaries offer to current and future church leaders;

4. to determine their interest in attending programs in the areas of leadership, stewardship, and management.

During the past ten years, DIAP seminars have demonstrated beyond any reasonable doubt that development can be both a profession and a ministry. According to the distinguished men and women who have worked with us in the past decade, development is a *profession* when it reflects the wisdom and experience of people who have devoted their working lives to perfecting their skills and to passing on their knowledge and values to others. Development is a *ministry* when it springs from the faith and enthusiasm of deeply religious people whose most basic motivation is not money but mission—the mission of theological education.

Thus, a development professional is one who is willing and able to learn from others and from his or her own mistakes. A development minister is one who recognizes that what people have to give is first and foremost *themselves,* and that good fund raising encourages the spiritual growth of donors at the same time that it promotes the responsible stewardship of church-related organizations.

Both stewardship and development are based on an essential underlying principle—namely, that it is good for people to give freely of their time, talent, and treasure. In scriptural terms stewardship and development take quite seriously the notions that one who sows bountifully will reap bountifully and that the best way to hold on to something is to give it away.

Those cynics who say that stewardship is merely a euphemism for fund raising have truly misunderstood the essential link between stewardship and the spiritual principles which are at the heart of Christian faith. Properly understood, stewardship is nothing less than Christian faith in action, or as John Westerhoff has said, "what we do after we say we believe." When it is properly done, stewardship education means calling the Christian community to a renewed understanding of the fact that there is a vital connection between what we say we believe and how we use our time, talent, and treasure on a daily basis.

Individuals are called to practice stewardship, and so are organizations. Indeed, the leaders of church-related organizations are called to exercise a special stewardship responsibility for the institutions and the resources which they oversee but which they do not own. Recent excesses of some TV evangelists and the financial crises facing nearly all of our mainline churches have sparked renewed interest in the stewardship responsibility which church leaders are called to exercise. But the practice of good stewardship goes much deeper than just the management of church funds, as important as this is for the well-being of churches. Good stewardship also is concerned with the quality of leadership itself and the priorities which church leaders establish in their use of the church's resources. To paraphrase the gospel, where our time, talent, and treasure are, there our hearts are also.

Similarly, those church-related organizations which have been slow to grasp the true significance of development as a means of stimulating, nurturing, and sustaining an institution's growth are missing a golden opportunity for revitalization and renewal. A truly effective development program does much more than raise money. Given the right combination of leadership within the institution and acceptance from carefully cultivated external constituencies, a successful development program can serve as the catalyst for the rebirth of organizations that are caught in the throes of institutional malaise.

Because good development forces an institution to reclaim its fundamental identity, to submit its case to the scrutiny of those who have no vested interest in the status quo, and to formulate plans that are truly worthy of investment, the process of development often seems like a "baptism by fire." A voluntary organization which survives the purgative fires of planning, communication, and fund raising emerges revitalized—not because of some secret recipe for success but because of the total process of clarifying mission and goals, reaching out to others, and accepting gifts of time, talent, and treasure from those who are true partners in the organization's mission.

Why are these reflections on stewardship and development significant for the church today? What do they have to do with the mission of theological education?

In the Stewardship and Development Study we asked pastors what their greatest area of frustration is. By an overwhelming majority they said "administration and money." When we asked pastors whether they thought that seminaries have a responsibility to teach students the *details* of managing local congregations, most of them said "yes."

When we asked seminary presidents, deans, and faculty the same question, their answer was quite different. Although they acknowledge the importance of these issues for pastors and local congregations, seminary personnel clearly said that "someone else" should teach church leaders how to be good stewards of their congregations' human, physical, and financial resources.

Why do seminaries think that it is someone else's job to teach leadership, stewardship, and management? Why isn't preparation for this very important dimension of pastoral ministry seen as an integral part of the mission of theological schools?

I can't think of a more appropriate place than a good theological school to help church leaders make the necessary connection between the things of the spirit and the things of the earth. Just because our seminaries are not currently prepared to teach the details of managing local congregations doesn't mean that it has to be this way. In fact, I think there are good reasons to believe that a seminary which commits itself to teaching present and future church leaders how to be good stewards will strengthen everything else that it does. Indeed, teaching leadership, stewardship, and management will help the school relate theological issues and concerns with the daily experience of individuals, families, and congregations.

What is it that church leaders need to know about leadership, stewardship, and management? What are the requirements of good stewardship? According to the people who were interviewed in the Stewardship and Development Study, a church leader is a good steward when he or she 1) is motivated by a personal commitment to the theology and practice of Christian stewardship, 2) has a profound sense of responsibility for the human, physical, and financial resources entrusted to his or her care, 3) is aware that his or her leadership is exercised on behalf of God, the true owner of all creation, and 4) either personally has the requisite leadership and management skills or can identify and recruit volunteers and staff who do possess these skills.

Note that the first three requirements for good stewardship have nothing to do with the professional skills that business leaders and nonprofit managers are taught in technical training programs. First and foremost, a good steward is someone who is thoroughly immersed in the religious values and theological principles which are the foundation for all expressions of leadership and service in the Christian community. Today, church leaders also need to be trained in the basic principles and skills of organizational leadership—those things that any leader with a mission, staff, and budget needs to know about leadership, management, and accountability.

Precisely because they are called to be leaders, clergy and lay people who are responsible for the resources of the church need to be comfortable overseeing the administrative and financial affairs of the congregation. Thus, while it is certainly not necessary to train church leaders in the technical aspects of management or finance, pastors and other church leaders should learn how to read a balance sheet, how to develop a long-range plan, and how to motivate people to give generously of their time, talent, and treasure in order to participate fully in the mission of the church.

The pastor who neglects the good order and financial well-being of the congregation because he or she feels burdened by management and money does the congregation and the ministry a real disservice. By accepting the dualistic fallacy which contends that money and management are not the pastor's responsibility, church leaders help to perpetuate two false ideas: 1) that there is a strict separation between the things of the spirit and the things of the earth, and 2) that religion is a private matter which is unconnected to the daily affairs of human society. This is not Christian faith, and it certainly is not good stewardship!

What does all of this have to do with us? Seminary development officers frequently have little or nothing to do with their school's curriculum or continuing education offerings. How can we hope to influence our school's attitudes toward training current and future leaders in the theology and practice of stewardship?

There is no easy answer to the question about what role, if any, you or I should play in all of this. I suspect that the answers vary from individual to individual and from institution to institution. Some seminary development officers have offered to teach courses in one or more of these areas. Others have collaborated with faculty, board members, or volunteers to design special programs for alums or local clergy. And still others have advocated for more research, discussion, and planning among seminaries, clergy groups, and denominational bodies in order to better respond to this urgent and increasingly complex problem.

I believe that the involvement of seminary development officers in the effort to make stewardship a "way of life" for individuals and for church-related organizations is good for the seminary and good for the church. Those of us who are called to provide leadership for the development function need to see ourselves as much more than marketing or fund raising technicians. We must be teachers and witnesses to the theology of stewardship as it is experienced concretely—in our personal lives and in our institutional responsibilities.

As with so many other things, the best way to teach good stewardship is by the example of good stewards. We who are convinced of the value of good stewardship (and of good development) need to be seen as people whose motivation is fundamentally different. For us the bottom line must always be growth—the spiritual growth of donors and the growth-in-mission of our institutions. We need to practice what we preach in all of our schools' development programs.

Wouldn't it be wonderful if in the year 2002—the twentieth anniversary of DIAP—attitudes about management and money would have changed dramatically? Suppose that in the year 2002 stewardship and development really were a way of life for each of us and for our Christian institutions. I am certain that our churches and our society would be much better places—not just because they would be better managed, but also because the spirit of generosity and sharing (the true spirit of stewardship) would have permeated all aspects of the church's life and mission.

The Theology of Money

Paul C. Reinert, SJ

I would like to explore with you various approaches to a Christian view of money, because I am sure you agree that a sound viewpoint on money is extremely important for seminarians and ministers, both in terms of their ability to be good stewards and in terms of their ability to be successful fund raisers.

Robert Wood Lynn suggests that ever since the Reformation stewardship has been used as a euphemism to cover up the embarrassment about money itself. Ministers have told him the three hardest sermons to preach are Christmas, Easter, and Stewardship Sunday. Typically, money has been a dirty word, and fund raising has been described pejoratively as begging or rattling the tin cup.

Preparing church leaders to exercise good stewardship requires developing a wholistic concept of leadership which embraces managerial responsibilities and the marshaling of resources needed to achieve the mission of the faith community.

What are some of the steps in developing such a concept? Let me suggest some thoughts on money from the *Spiritual Exercises* of St. Ignatius Loyola, the founder of the Jesuits 450 years ago. In his opening meditations Ignatius establishes the relationship between God, the Creator, and humankind, the crown of creation. Then he turns to all the other creatures in the world and he defines them basically as means to help humans achieve salvation and union with the Creator for all eternity. Creatures, including money, are intended by God to be helps, depending on how we use them.

Life is a welter of possibilities: to be rich, to be wretched, to be powerful, to be marginated, to marry, to be single, to be healthy, to be sickly. Whenever a concrete choice is presented, I must try to hold my desiring and my choosing in abeyance until I can see in each concrete particular what leads me toward God and what leads me away from God. Anything that leads me away from God I resolutely repudiate; anything that may please or help me personally, yet leaves me loving God and my fellow human beings less, I should drop. The English translation of the Spanish word Ignatius used to describe this contrast of our choices is *indifference,* but this is not the best word as commonly understood today. What is called for is objectivity, a balance, a poise, the ability to weigh the consequences before I make a free choice. I think it is quite easy to see how this Ignatian principle can and should be used in respect to money. There is nothing intrinsically morally good or bad about money. It is a creature that can help or hinder me in my service of God and those around me. I use it, I guard it, I seek it *if* it can help me in my ministry or mission. I avoid it if it will tarnish or sever my filial relationship with God and potential relationships with those who depend on me.

Second, I believe this Ignatian principle: use of all creatures insofar as they lead me to God and rejection of them insofar as they hold me back is clearly founded on Scripture and the teachings of Christ. In the parable of the talents, for example, Jesus deliberately used a money unit as a symbol of a creature capable of growth and increased value to teach the lesson not only of valuing the gifts of God but of our accountability—an essential feature, incidentally, in our stewardship role.

Now I'd like to move to a broader concept of money—a theological concept of thinking about and dealing with money as a ministry, a spiritual calling. I urge that we include fund raising in the same sacred categories as preaching, shepherding, sacramental ministry, healing, reconciling—all Christian works of mercy and charity. Not only can dealing with money be a ministry, but it can and should be a sacred service to three categories of persons:

1. the steward, manager, development officer;
2. the donor, giver, benefactor;
3. the receiver, recipient, beneficiary.

Let's begin with the first category. Based on forty years of fund raising, I am convinced that one called to raise money for the church, for spreading the gospel, for religious education, can and should enjoy a wonderfully blessed ministry. He or she will be successful to the extent that four spiritual qualities are present:

1. Commitment to the cause, and especially to the people the cause represents, to volunteer workers and to the donors themselves. Any fund raiser worth his or her salt can put the needs of an institution in an impressive slide presentation, but what can never be put in pictures or brochures is his or her own deep-down personal commitment to the cause.

2. Genuine enthusiasm, not a psyched-up Madison Avenue sort of showmanship, but an abiding, persevering sense of privilege that one has the joy of perpetuating and enhancing something that is destined to improve the quality of human lives.

3. A spirit of unselfishness. If a fund raiser is honestly committed to the cause, he or she could care less who receives the credit and kudos for getting the job done. I've seen the desire for self-aggrandizement in a fund raiser work successfully for a while, but eventually he or she alienates either the donors or the employers, or both.

4. A deep, lasting humility and resilience. Asking persons for money whose wealth has made them arrogant or cynical frequently becomes a heroic act. There are people who are so crass that they try to make you crawl to them for some form of help. No one likes to be turned down, but it hurts to be turned down for a bogus reason.

These four inseparable qualities—commitment, enthusiasm, unselfishness, and resilient humility—all add up to the spiritual essence of philanthropy in the person of the fund raiser, the motivator of the process. I feel that the successful fund raiser is such precisely because his or her work has taken on the characteristic of a ministry.

I firmly believe that the entire fund raising process has been clearly elevated to the status of a ministry from the very beginning of Christianity. For example, the apostle Paul himself begs as part of his apostolate; he requires and praises the same in his followers such as Barnabas and Titus. As he encourages his different flocks to vie with each other in generosity, he insists that those coming to them for this purpose are doing so in a spiritual capacity: "Brothers, I should like you to know of the grace of God conferred on the churches of Macedonia. In the midst of severe trial their overflowing joy and deep poverty have produced an abundant generosity. According to their means—indeed I can testify even beyond their means—and voluntarily, they begged us insistently for the favor of sharing this service to the members of the church."

Now to move to the second category. I have seen wonders occur in all three components of the fund raising process, but by far the greatest spiritual miracles I have personally witnessed have occurred in this second group of persons now under scrutiny—the potential and actual donors.

While there is usually a more identifiable motive for making a gift, I think that many donors are finally moved by a spiritual motivation so personal and so subtle that they would not mention it in response to a questionnaire even if they knew how to express it.

Let me try to explain what I feel this spiritual motivation is by describing what I have seen happen in many a real-life situation. There are plenty of individuals who are hoarding their assets, concerned only with themselves, their immediate family, and the pleasures and honors which their wealth makes available. Their interests are fundamentally egotistical and self-centered. The first step is to get them personally interested in something outside themselves and their tight-knit business concerns. A fund raiser may set out to try to bring such individuals to an understanding of the problems and needs of young people who do not have resources, but who honestly want an opportunity to do something meaningful in life by acquiring an education.

This triggers a gradual process of self-discovery, a process within the prospective donor's own personality which can be truly remarkable. In many cases, one's interests will broaden by the month; he or she will begin to realize that giving brings with it a deep sense of personal satisfaction, that by and large people are extremely grateful for a helping hand, and that generosity leads to civic leadership and deserved recognition for qualities much more highly regarded than inherited wealth or raw power. To make a long story short, such a person, largely because he or she was motivated to become a generous giver, is a fundamentally better, more beloved person than he or she otherwise would ever have become.

And the third category. Although we often miss it in our fund raising efforts, I think that there is a deep spiritual significance and value for the recipient of our efforts even though we may think of the recipient as an institution, a program, or something impersonal. This is where we make our mistake. True, there is no spiritual essence in an institution itself. But these are not the recipients in the vast majority of our efforts. In most of the campaigns worth devoting our time to, it is human beings who are the ultimate objectives and recipients. The spiritual essence of philanthropy insofar as the receiver is concerned lies in the fact that we are doing something good, something important for people.

There you have it—as a religious fund raiser you can be involved in a highly idealistic, spiritual vocation which involves every aspect and person in the fund raising process: the fund raiser, the donor, and the beneficiary.

That sublimates the whole process from science to art and to ministry. How fortunate can a fund raiser be?

Seminary Development as a Model for Ministry

Donald R. Cooney

Lay persons who serve as development officers at theological seminaries enjoy immunity from at least one affliction suffered by their ordained colleagues in this profession: laity are rarely, if ever, asked whether they have any plans to return to the ministry.

Although it is commonplace for seminary development officers to describe much or all of their work as "ministry," I have encountered very few others who describe the functions of a development officer in this way. This is true even though most persons seem to presume that a seminary development officer is an ordained seminary graduate.

All clergy who are engaged in ministry beyond the local church are subject to a popular skepticism of the validity and appropriateness of their work in relation to their ordination. But by the very nature of their work, seminary development officers are presented with a special opportunity to address this skepticism and, in the process, provide a needed service to their church.

The opportunity is not limited to defending seminary development officers against charges of coercive huckstering and pocket picking, or to arguing on behalf of a legitimate place for development in the enterprise of theological education, or even to disseminating winsome accounts of people helped to become better stewards of God's gifts (while cutting taxes on capital gains, too!). The real opportunity is to make the case that seminary development is not only ministry, but is in fact a model for effective ministry in our times.

This opportunity is especially pronounced for development officers in the seminaries of mainline Protestantism. The officers at these institutions are in a unique position to model ministry where mainline churches are with ever greater frequency called to be: on the periphery.

As the mainline moves to the sideline, from main street to the side street, from being a voice of influence to a voice in the wilderness, the development officers of seminaries can model a ministry that has learned to live in the reality of marginalization.

Seminary development officers really do function on the periphery of the development profession. Let me suggest three illustrations of our life on the margin.

1. Seminary development officers minister in institutions at the margin of higher education. Size alone assures this: our institutions are small. Last spring *The Chronicle of Higher Education* described as "tiny" a college with an enrollment five times that of my seminary. Another university recently announced a reduction in staff over the next years, to be achieved by attrition alone, which will exceed the number of persons on our entire payroll—plus our entire student body.

Development programs in higher education mirror this scale. It would be a major advance for my seminary to realize $15 million in gift income during the next five years. For many institutions, that total represents a few major gifts. Large campaigns are identified not by the millions, but by the billions, raised. Objective analysts rightly wonder how our institutions survive with our precarious funding and narrowly focused missions.

Our fragile institutions are not likely to set the agenda for discussion in this kind of environment. Adapting to changing demographics and emerging social realities continues to consume much of the energy of seminaries and their development officers. This requires the seminary development officer to be an interpreter of change much more often than an agent of change.

2. Seminary development officers are required to be generalists in a specialized profession. Once again, the size of the institution plays a determinative role in the marginalization of the seminary development officer. Last year I attended a grant writing seminar where I met persons in full-time positions with responsibility for a single step in the process of generating grant proposals at their institutions. Seminary resources simply are not adequate to employ one person to do research, another to schedule submissions, another to prepare preliminary drafts, another to interact with faculty and grantors.

While the breadth of responsibility brings variety and challenge to the work of the seminary development officer, it also takes away opportunities to be influential in a given field. If on any given day I may be called upon to interpret an alternative minimum tax computation, to analyze the return rates on a direct mail piece, to evaluate the time and setting for a cultivation event, to screen volunteer leadership for a discreet phase in a capital campaign, and to interpret the nuances of our relationship with a denominational judicatory, the opportunity to develop extensive skills in any one of these areas is limited. Much of the challenge of the work is to keep pace with advances in each of these disciplines while being an effective steward of current and prospective donors.

3. *Even in the church, seminary development officers minister in unwelcome territory.* Two factors are at work here. For the most part, North American Christians continue to be perplexed over what to do with their abundant prosperity. This is not solely a matter of uncertainty about stewardship; it also reflects ambiguity in our attitudes toward money. These confusions around wealth are exacerbated by the second factor: the low esteem with which fund raisers—and hence, by extension, seminary development officers—are held by society at large and especially by church members. If the church has difficulty understanding money and how to deal with it, those who traffic in it pose an even more difficult challenge for the church to understand.

In these three ways, the seminary development officer ministers on the margin: on the margin in the industry of higher education dominated by much larger and much more elite institutions; on the margin in a profession which displays ever-increasing specialization; on the margin in a church that continues to fumble in its incapacity to deal with wealth.

But it is precisely these realities which give to the seminary development officer the "peripheral vision" to be a model for ministry for the church that finds itself living on the margin of society. Ministers in local churches, be they clergy or laity, address the same issues of marginalization faced by the seminary development officer.

1. *Ministers in the local church function in institutions which have ceased to be a dominating force in many communities.* Like their counterparts in theological education, these ministers act more as interpreters of change than agents of change.

2. *Ministers in the local church are required to be generalists in a society which values specialization.* When I ask members of search committees to identify the skills they are looking for in their next pastor, I frequently hear "good preacher, good administrator, good theologian, good with youth, good at pastoral counseling, good in leading worship, good in hospital visitation, good at life's transitions, good at church growth, good in Christian education, good at social occasions, with a good spouse." These good people cannot afford the luxury of specialization and hope to meet this range of expectations.

3. *Ministers in the local church often minister in unwelcome territory.* This includes, but is not limited to, that issue of money and what to do with it. Other sensitive issues also pervade the current discourse in the church, such as sexuality, racism, justice and peace. In addition to meeting all other expectations, the local minister is called upon to deal adroitly with these issues, often within a congregation reluctant to face the tough questions they raise.

Ministers in the local church must also have a "peripheral vision" as they go about their work. I am convinced that the development of theological seminaries is a ministry, and indeed a significant one. One form that ministry can take is to allow our experiences in ministry on the margin to support and sustain others in distinct, but comparable, ministries.

Social trends notwithstanding, the generalist who tackles the tough issues on the edges of the debate can make a radical difference in the human experience. And all of us know a perfect model for that ministry.

A Development Officer
Looks at Stewardship

David Heetland

I find that a theology of stewardship increasingly influences my work as a development officer. I am attracted to the words in 1 Peter 4:10 as a wonderful summary of what I'd like my ministry to be: we are to be "good stewards of God's varied grace" (RSV). Or, as stated in some other versions, we are called to be "responsible handlers" (The Cotton Patch Version), "good managers" (TEV), "faithful dispensers of the magnificently varied grace of God" (J. B. Phillips). If I had to put it in my own words I would say we are called to be caretakers of God's undeserved love. Our calling is not simply to receive God's undeserved love for ourselves, but to demonstrate God's caring love to all of creation.

This, of course, has wide-ranging implications for every aspect of our lives: how, as caretakers, we "take care" of our environment, our bodies, our sisters and brothers, our time, our talents, our treasure. A theology of stewardship needs to be understood in the broadest possible terms if it is to have the necessary power to change lives.

Having said that, I must quickly add that the focus of my words is on only one aspect of stewardship: stewardship of financial resources, as this is the primary focus of our ministries. How, then, does a theology of stewardship influence my work as a development officer? Let me cite a few ways:

First, a theology of stewardship helps me see each person as a child of God. A donor or prospective donor is a whole person, an important part of God's creation regardless of financial resources. He or she is not a means to an end, someone to be manipulated for some "greater purpose." A theology of stewardship reminds me that donors should not be regarded or referred to as Mrs. Bigbucks or Mr. Deeppockets but as full human beings who may have the gift of financial resources along with many other varied gifts.

Second, a theology of stewardship invites me to know and appreciate these people in their fullness, so that I can be a more responsible caretaker of their gifts. A theology of stewardship encourages me to develop relationships of mutual care and respect for all God's creation. Thus, my relationship with donors and potential donors is not so much a "one shot" attempt to "get a gift" as it is a long-term commitment to know them as persons, with their own unique needs and aspirations. It is only when I come to understand as fully as possible what their hopes and values are that I can be a "good manager of God's different gifts," bringing together the dreams of donors and the goals of an institution.

Third, a theology of stewardship helps me understand my role as a development officer. I am not a "professional beggar" whose job is to extricate a gift from an unwilling donor, but rather a minister whose vocation is to provide opportunities and invite responses. It has been suggested that the lack of financial resources is the major impediment to eradicating hunger, developing self-help programs, and spreading the gospel of Jesus Christ. What could be more rewarding than being "faithful dispensers of the magnificently varied grace of God," enabling ministries of relief, development, and proclamation to be carried out in Christ's name by helping to provide adequate resources?

Fourth, a theology of stewardship helps me recognize that if I am to be a "responsible handler of God's many-sided grace" my invitations to give must reflect God's own nature. Such invitations, in other words, should reflect genuine care for the donor, compassion, integrity, honesty. They should not reflect greed, fear, or guilt. And, of course, they must respect the donor's right to say "yes" or "no" to the invitation.

I would guess your work in development is influenced by a similar understanding of stewardship. However, I'm sure we all know ministers who want nothing to do with the stewardship of financial resources. These persons look at the development of financial resources as dirty work, something beneath their calling and less important than other ministerial tasks. Such an attitude boggles my mind, especially given Jesus' own emphasis on the subject. But the fallout is much greater than simply my boggled mind. Look with me for a moment at what happens when our graduates fail to develop a theology of stewardship which places a high priority on the stewardship of financial resources.

First and foremost, the work of the church is diminished. The church has barely tapped its full financial potential—largely because people in the church have not been adequately informed, inspired, or invited to give. Some sobering research has been done by empty tomb, inc., suggesting that while the incomes of church members are rising, the percentage given to the church is declining. I believe ministers must face the fact that they have played a role in this decline by abdicating their role as strong leaders in financial stewardship.

A second fallout is missed opportunities for spiritual growth. Many church people do not see their pattern of giving related in any meaningful way to their own spiritual growth. An essential part of the Christian message, however, proclaims that the two are intricately related. When this message is not taught boldly and with conviction, members often are not motivated to grow in their giving and an important part of their spiritual growth is stunted.

A third fallout is that the lack of church leaders willing to emphasize financial stewardship creates a vacuum which is quickly filled by charlatans. Such persons do not seek gifts based on a theology of stewardship. Rather they prey on the unwary and the unwise, using tactics of manipulation and coercion, seeking to motivate gifts through guilt, greed, and fear. I think little more needs to be said by me on this point. There are plenty of examples in recent years to remind us all that such charlatans exist and that unfortunately people respond. One can only wonder if they would be so prone to respond if they were grounded in a strong theology of stewardship.

Thus, the critical question becomes, "How do we teach seminarians and ministers the importance of stewardship?" I would hope our seminaries would develop comprehensive models of stewardship training which would incorporate some or all of the following:

First, a stewardship emphasis in existing courses. A number of seminary professors already do this. Could all professors be encouraged to consider this? Stewardship could be explored in biblical courses, history courses, preaching courses, theology courses. In fact, I can think of no seminary course where a study of stewardship would not be appropriate.

Second, a new course in stewardship. I know all the reasons why not to add new courses to the curriculum. I also know a perfectly good reason for doing so: such a course is needed! I regularly hear from both clergy and laity saying they wish such a course were offered. A course in stewardship might well serve as an integrating course, bringing together the insights from various disciplines, and helping students see that a stewardship lifestyle represents a summing-up of the meaning of a religious life: that Christian love means a solidarity with the earth and all God's creation, and a commitment to devote our time, talents, and resources to preserving and improving both.

Third, continuing education courses in stewardship. Recently a denominational executive wanted to take a continuing education course in stewardship, and was disappointed to discover that none of his denominational seminaries offered anything in this area. Oftentimes ministers are most receptive to stewardship courses after they have been practicing ministry for some time. Thus, it is critical to offer periodic continuing education courses in this area.

Fourth, a lecture series on some aspect of stewardship. Many seminaries have a week of lectures or some similar format. A fairly frequent complaint from practicing clergy, however, is that the lectures do not address their most pressing concerns. I cannot think of a lecture series that would be more relevant to most church leaders than that of stewardship, and exploring the implications of stewardship for one's ministry and one's life.

Fifth, opportunities to practice stewardship. This may well be the most important—and the most difficult to implement. We all know that we learn best by doing rather than by simply hearing, and that we are most likely to make changes in our lives if we are supported by others making similar changes. Thus, the communities in which we live and work could provide daily opportunities for us to practice—as well as discuss—stewardship. Covenant groups and action groups could be encouraged which would help our communities prophetically address what it means to be a steward in today's world.

Let me conclude by issuing a radical suggestion. I would like to suggest for your thinking that perhaps our most important responsibility as development officers is not to raise funds for our institutions. Rather, perhaps our most important responsibility is to raise awareness of what it means to be a responsible steward. If we as development officers would take the leadership in helping incorporate one or more of these ideas into our respective institutions, we would, I think, be moving in the right direction toward developing more committed and effective leaders in stewardship. I can think of no greater gift that we could give the church.

Chapter Two:
Fund Raising Basics

Acres of Diamonds Revisited

Chase S. Hunt

It was well over a century ago that a Turkish guide, persisting in his efforts to impress and entertain a young American tourist with tales of local tradition and lore, reached into his barrel of legends for one more try. The traveler had been unimpressed thus far, even contemptuous of the guide's attempts to amuse him and impart bits of wisdom through these stories. It was only because he was a captive audience that he resigned himself to endure yet another yarn.

This one had to do with a wealthy Persian farmer, Al Hafed by name. Influenced by stories told him by a Buddhist monk who visited his farm one day, Al Hafed sold his farm, left his family with a neighbor, and set out in search of a diamond mine and the greater influence such wealth would bring him. It was an ill-fated quest, however, for although he had roamed far and wide, Al Hafed died many years later in a distant land a poor, disillusioned, dispirited man.

In the meantime, the guide continued, back on the farm, Al Hafed's successor led his camel to drink from a garden brook. In the process, he was impressed by a curious flash of light that shone through the clear water from the sands of the shallow stream. Reaching down, he removed a black stone with an eye of light that reflected brilliantly and left it on a table in his house. A few days later, the same priest who had visited the farm when Al Hafed owned it returned once more and recognized the stone to be a diamond. Hurrying back outside, the two of them dug through the white sands with their fingers and found other diamonds more valuable and beautiful than the first. There, on the very land Al Hafed had forsaken, were discovered the diamond mines of Golconda.

The guide had finally succeeded in piercing the resistance the unwilling American listener had to his tales and for that traveler, Russell Conwell, this one became life changing. It persuaded him to resist any temptation to look for the "diamonds" of life in distant places and to concentrate on unearthing them right where he was. He was thus led to become ordained and to rebuild a bankrupt church in Lexington, Massachusetts, then to take a struggling church in Philadelphia and revitalize it, and eventually to become the founder of Temple University. He also shared the ancient story told him by his Turkish guide and the significance it held for him with others through his lecture, "Acres of Diamonds." In it, he encouraged the hearer to "do what you can with what you have where you are today." It struck such a responsive chord with audiences that he delivered it from platform and on radio more than six thousand times and, in the course of doing so, raised some $7 million.

My thought in relating this incident is that I believe there is an essential validity in Conwell's insight that has application for those of us engaged in development for the theological institutions we serve and that we should take to heart. This is not intended in a narrow sense, for I would be as quick as the next person to go at a moment's notice to points near and far to meet with a prospect or donor on behalf of my seminary. It is to say, however, that while there is a certain glamour and sense of excitement associated with such events, particularly when they result in a gift, it is the disciplined, faithful cultivation and servicing of those nearest us that represent the "acres of diamonds" for our institutions.

The nearness to which I refer is not only in terms of physical proximity, although it surely includes that, but in terms of relationship to the institution as well. We are talking, then, about our neighbors, both residential and those in our business community, trustees, faculty, administrative staff, alums, and other friends of our schools.

When I think of those who are neighbors and friends from the local community, a number of things come to mind. One is our practice at the seminary I serve of publicizing through the media special services of worship, lectures, musical and dramatic presentations, and other events that we feel would be of interest. Personal invitations are also extended when that seems appropriate and, on occasion, combined with a dinner or reception. Our neighbors also feel welcome to make use of the resources of our library.

In the fall of the year, we have a Saturday morning event to which alums and friends within a radius of about seventy-five miles of the seminary are invited. On that occasion, our president speaks on a topic of his choosing and a faculty member makes a presentation in an area of his or her expertise. At the conclusion of the formal program, a picnic lunch is served and a number of options are offered for the afternoon that include a campus tour, visiting the seminary bookstore, attending a Princeton University football game, or simply enjoying the resources of the campus or the town. This event has been well received, and we are encouraged by the fact that each year it attracts new as well as old friends to our campus.

We are experiencing considerable population growth in the Princeton area of both the residential and business communities. We relate to the latter through the local chamber of commerce, and earlier this year invited that group to have one of their luncheon meetings on our campus. A number of students and spouses are employed by local firms, which gives further opportunity for linkage to occur and for a heightened awareness of the seminary on the part of these firms in a more personal way.

Sometimes opportunities to reach out and relate to an institution's neighbors present themselves unexpectedly. One such opportunity came to our seminary when a local church was engaged in extensive renovation and was interested in having an alternative place in which to worship during that period. Our chapel was an ideal answer to their need, and we were pleased to make it available to that congregation.

The manner in which our institutions relate to their trustees, faculty, and staff is a rather personal matter—something of a family affair. I would venture to say, however, that common to all of our institutions in our dealings with trustees, faculty, and staff are the importance of clear and effective communications, a sense of mission and common purpose, a respect for the particular role of each one on the part of the others, and the helpfulness of all in suggesting the names of prospective donors and in assisting to cultivate their interest. In recent years, the trustees, faculty, and staff had the experience of developing a new mission statement for our institution. This was a significant experience for all of us and enhanced our appreciation of each other and of our seminary as a whole. I am convinced that a feeling of involvement and participation among those who serve the institution in these capacities is essential if support is to come and the institution prosper.

What is true of the way in which our institutions relate to trustees, faculty, and staff is no less true of our relationship with our alums. Clear, informative communications with our graduates are essential and can be carried out on many levels, from a personal conversation or letter, on the one hand, to publications and other printed materials on the other. Our primary source of communication with alums is through a quarterly magazine that offers class notes, news, and feature stories about the seminary and its graduates and their respective ministries. A number of alum meetings are scheduled each year in various parts of the country (and occasionally overseas) that feature a presentation by our president and/or a member of the faculty. This means of alum contact is being enhanced by a network of alum chapters currently being established throughout the country and beyond.

Our annual giving program for alums also serves as a valuable means of communication about the seminary, its hopes and dreams and needs. Mailings from the seminary are reinforced by brief notes written by a network of volunteer alums, each one writing to ten classmates. This has brought about a growing response in alum giving during the three years this particular program has been in use. In addition, a number of contacts have been reestablished on a personal level through the writing of these notes, much to the delight of the particular alum involved.

All of these reflect a continuing effort to have open lines of communication with our alums in both directions; a clear interpretation of our school's mission, program, and vision for the future; and an appreciation of and respect for our alums and the ministries in which they are engaged. When these exist, financial support and personal participation follow as an expression of common purpose and pride in the institution.

Other friends of our schools, by which I mean donors and prospective donors who are not alums, require and look to us for similar care. Since they are not graduates of our institutions, the need for communication is even more crucial if they are to understand what we are about, catch the vision we have for our schools, and make the decision to give us their support and become partners with us in our mission. We have sought for many years now to keep our non-alum constituency informed about the seminary through a quarterly publication prepared with them in mind. It has recently been revised in both format and content, and we trust that it will serve our institution and our readers well. We, of course, have a variety of other contacts with our friends through letters, telephone calls, and personal visits.

We are careful to identify those among both alums and non-alums who seem to be likely candidates for our planned giving program, and mail materials describing the various planned giving arrangements available through our seminary to them periodically. We also advertise the planned giving opportunities we offer in a variety of publications, and are quick to respond when inquiries are received or other indications of interest are evident.

Being a firm believer in the axiom "the first gift is neither the largest nor the last," I work at making regular contact with the most promising donors of record, especially those with planned giving potential or who have already entered into a planned giving arrangement with our school. Such calls are made for a number of reasons and not only when a gift is anticipated. They are made, for example, to express thanks for their interest and concern for the seminary, to be sure they are pleased with the service they receive from us, and, in the process, to listen with care to whatever they may have to say. I find this exceedingly helpful and believe it is genuinely appreciated by those individuals.

In looking, then, to serve and develop the continuing interest of those near our institutions, both in proximity and in affection, it is clear that there are certain essentials that should be operative. These include good communication, thoughtfully prepared and presented at whatever level; a current statement of the institution's mission, program, vision, and needs; a genuine concern for and appreciation of our constituents; a disciplined program of cultivation and service for those who have taken an interest in and identified themselves with our institutions; and adequate opportunities and means made available to them to give to our schools the benefit of their support. With these in place and due diligence on our part, we should, indeed, find the acres of diamonds that were so elusive to Al Hafed.

What I Wish I Had Known Last Year: Reflections on a Development Officer's First Year

F. Stuart Gulley

February 1, 1990, I was like the proverbial fish out of water. I was the new director of development for the Candler School of Theology. Excited by the challenge, I was stymied by my inexperience. From every quarter of the university, persons were generous with their offers of assistance, but I did not even know what to ask. I knew my job was to raise money, but how? Previously, I had recruited students for the school, but that task seemed a far cry from raising $400,000 for the annual fund. One year later, I have a little better handle on the situation. As I look back, five areas occur to me as being both helpful and important in my first year. They seem obvious now, but I wish someone had told me about them last year. I share them here in the hope that the new development officer or the CEO with a new development officer will be helped by them.

Visit, visit, visit. The Nike commercial admonishes us to "Just do it," and that is true with development visits. Nothing is more enjoyable or more necessary for securing the gift. Once you start you will relish meeting your donors, hearing their stories, learning of their commitments to the church, and working with them to insure that future ministers receive the very finest theological education. In planning your visits, you might consider the following:

In consultation with your superiors, determine a reasonable number of visits for you to conduct each month and use this number as your goal. At Emory, all development officers are expected to make a minimum of sixteen (soon to be increased to twenty and eventually to twenty-five) visits per month. This is a manageable number, but it has meant being on the road fifty percent of the time. I also set as a goal meeting all of our major donors in the first year. Through strategic planning, I was able to meet most donors in thirteen months.

Maintain files that divide your donors by state. These state files will be invaluable in your travel planning. Once you learn of prospective donors, place their names in the appropriate state file so you will remember to visit them on your next trip to that area.

Set aside time each week for visit planning. During this time, look ahead to the next two weeks and determine your travel plans and whom you will visit. Contact your donors by phone to make arrangements. I have found arranging visits more than two weeks ahead of time is too soon for most donors, and to wait until less than one week ahead of time is too short. Seven to fourteen days ahead of time seems to work well.

Don't forget to arrange visits with alums and area pastors when possible. These persons are just as valuable as your large donors. They can help tell the institution's story, and they have access to prospective donors.

When traveling, stay in the homes of donors. It's cheaper for the institution, and it establishes a stronger and closer bond with the donor.

All of your visits don't have to be off campus. Occasionally bring a donor or prospective donor to the campus. Introduce them to students and faculty. Show them your facilities and serve them a meal. A successful visit will bring them even closer to your institution.

Visit your faculty regularly. Your faculty is an important ingredient in the success of your institution and support of your work. Arrange to have coffee or lunch with them individually. Tell them about your work, but most importantly listen to their perceptions of your institution.

Know who your LYBUNTS are and follow up. This area overlaps with the previous one, but it is so crucial it deserves separate mention. It took me ten weeks to learn that LYBUNTS means "Last Year (giver) But Unfortunately Not This." Then it took ten more weeks to realize I needed to review the previous year's financial record, and by comparing it to this year's record identify those persons who have not repeated their gifts. We did not make our goal last year, but giving in the last quarter was one of the highest ever because we focused on our LYBUNTS by visiting, phoning, or writing them.

Plan ahead and manage the details of events; don't let the details slip up and manage you. Small and large donor events require the same attention and care. After several hard-learned lessons, we devised the following checklist to guide us in our event planning:

Confirm in writing date of event with all parties.
Arrange parking.
Select menu.
Reserve room(s).
Plan program and arrange speakers.
Arrange for set-up of public address system.
Decide on flowers and place cards.
Prepare news release or announcement.
Secure photographer.

After the event, the following checklist applies:
Write letters of thanks to everyone involved.
Send photographs to donors as a gift.
Send photographs to appropriate church papers.
Thank your staff and maintenance workers.

Read voraciously. Being a novice, I wanted to learn as much as possible about fund raising, alum affairs, and institutional advancement, and finding reading material on these subjects was not a problem. Books I found particularly helpful included Gurin's *Confessions of a Fundraiser,* Panas' *Born to Raise,* Seymour's *Designs for Fund-Raising,* Johnson and Wilson's *The One Minute Salesperson,* and Zuker's *The Assertive Manager.*

Order a CASE catalogue. There you will find loads of

resources about direct mail, phonathons, the annual fund, and so forth. You might consider subscribing to the *Fundraising Institute Monthly Portfolio* as well as *Currents.* And by all means, write for back issues of *Seminary Development News.*

Don't forget to read up on your institution's history. I had been at Candler for six years prior to coming to this position and had not taken the time to read our history. Our history book was full of useful information and helped me understand better how we got where we are today.

Hold regular meetings and take time for a planning retreat. On my desk I maintain two lists at all times. They are headed "Agenda for Dean's Meeting" and "Agenda for Staff Meeting." As items and issues that need to be discussed in these meetings occur to me, I can easily add them to the list and not worry that I will forget them. Weekly meetings with the associate director, biweekly meetings with the dean, and tri-weekly meetings with the entire development team have been important to keep me current and to implement the development plan.

In mid-summer, the associate director and I packed our bags and files and headed thirty minutes outside Atlanta to a small retreat center. We stayed there three days evaluating our work and planning our efforts for the next giving year. On day two my predecessor joined us for feedback and advice, and on day three our support staff joined us for more reflection and planning. The result was a twenty-five-page working document, complete with calendar, outlining our plans for 1990-91. This document has been crucial in guiding our efforts. It serves as the agenda for our staff meetings and will be important for our evaluation of the overall program which we will undertake once again this summer.

After one short year, I certainly don't consider myself an expert. Each day I am learning new approaches and strategies. I know the above list is incomplete, but I hope these reflections spur the newcomer to overcome any hesitations and to dive head-first with confidence into this exciting work.

Ten Steps to
an Annual Fund Action Plan

Mark A. Holman

An annual fund by any other name is still an annual fund. Whether your seminary's definition includes only unrestricted gifts or all gifts for current purposes, whether it includes church support or only individual gifts, the bottom line is this: all seminaries depend on multiple constituencies to provide sources of income to meet operating budget requirements. A solid annual fund plan clearly recognizes these various sources and develops specific strategies for each. Good planning is essential. Consider the following suggestions and questions.

1. Start planning early. Although it is unwise to sacrifice fiscal year-end efforts at the altar of advance planning for next year, it is equally dangerous to wait for Christmas to begin plotting a strategy for a fiscal year by then half-gone. Make an appointment with yourself to start the process.

2. Review last year's goals and accomplishments. What goals were set? How? Why? Were the goals for the annual fund program (perhaps including alum relations) related to overall departmental and seminary-wide goals? Was the annual fund target met? Why or why not? Be critical in your evaluation.

3. Analyze your donor base. Just as in a major gifts campaign, it is important to develop a gift range chart for the annual fund. Ask yourself: How many gifts at what levels have made up this year's annual fund? What percentage came from which constituencies? How do these amounts and percentages compare to the previous year? What is the rate of renewal, lapse, and new donor acquisition at each gift level? What is the story behind each of the large lapsed gifts?

4. Analyze your strategies. How did you segment your appeals? Based on giving history (LYBUNT, PYBUNT,

SYBUNT, Never-Giver)? Based on constituency (board, advisory council, faculty/staff, alums, student/alum families, congregations, church groups, corporations, foundations, matching grant programs)? By some combination of these? What were your strategies for each of your segments? Why did each succeed or fail? What forms of contact were employed (phone, mail, visits)? Were the appropriate persons involved? Was the appropriate message conveyed to each constituency as the "case" for their supporting your mission and ministry? What follow-up stewardship strategies were employed to recognize donors and cultivate their continuing interest?

5. Analyze your budget. How much money was spent on each strategy or segment? Was the amount invested proportional to the amount received? How much was spent on new donor acquisition, current donor and top prospect cultivation and solicitation, top donor recognition? Did you stay within budget? What are your budget restrictions for next year?

6. Analyze your use of time. How much time did you spend on each strategy or segment? How much time was spent making personal contact with your donors? If too much time was spent "behind the scenes" preparing mailings and the like, consider alternative division-of-labor strategies. Is student assistance available? Volunteers from local church auxiliaries? Can you involve current donors in your work?

7. Write your plan. Analyzing your past efforts as suggested above is crucial, but there's no substitute for sitting down to start writing. Make an appointment with yourself. Don't worry about a first-draft masterpiece. Where is the greatest potential for growth next year? Start there. Then list other segments and jot down ideas for strategies. Let your imagination be your guide.

Put the list away for a couple days and set aside a full day away from the office to write. Begin with a brief overview of what needs to happen to reach next year's annual fund goal. Include numerical comparisons between last year's actual and next year's projected figures—by constituency and gift level—to support your points. Also provide comparative budget figures.

Conclude with a timeline for implementing and coordinating your strategies.

Finally, present a draft of your plan to your supervisor and your colleagues for input and discussion. Make sure all understand how your plans will impact their work—and vice-versa.

8. Develop an annual fund prospect list. This is a concrete extension of your gift range chart. Who (by name) are your prospects for renewal and upgrade, especially at the top levels? Who are your prospects for new gifts? Develop for each of the major annual fund prospects a strategy which considers the "who? how? when? how much?" of major gift solicitations. Set an initial meeting and regularly scheduled briefings with those involved in the asks to track progress on each strategy. In most cases, the top twenty percent (or less) of your donors will provide eighty percent (or more) of your income. Focusing on your top prospect list is time well spent.

9. Work your plan. A well-conceived, well-written plan is of little use when it sits in the drawer. Review your plan each month to see that you're on track with your timeline. Look ahead to future months and ask what adjustments might be made to your initial strategy. Make a gift range progress report and a prospect "moves" update part of your monthly gift reporting. Regular review of your plan can help prevent unpleasant surprises at fiscal year-end.

10. Keep an idea file for next year. As you or those you work with come up with useful ideas for future strategies, write these ideas down! It is helpful to start an idea file for next year as part of this year's planning and implementation process. Every brainstorm can make next year's planning a little easier. Planning is a fixed-time exercise, but it is also an ongoing process. Keep ahead of the game!

Alums Are Friends First

Frank A. Mullen

Being director of development at Yale University Divinity School is one of the most fun jobs in the United States. My office is across the courtyard from the dorm where I first lived as a student in 1953. To have advanced only fifty feet in thirty-five years is not much progress, but—*c'est la vie!*

I have a wonderful dean with whom to work and 6,787 alums for whom to work. The dean and I have tried to establish a "climate of giving" for our constituency. We have worked intentionally to enable people (graduates and others) to find "the joy of giving." Many people simply have never discovered this. How sad. To give 'til it helps is a far cry from to give 'til it hurts.

The dean and I think of our alums not as money machines but as *friends*. If we think of alums *first* as potential donors, we are in trouble. Alums are the most important people in the world as far as the development/alum office is concerned. Alums are not dependent upon us—we are dependent on them. Alums are not an interruption of our work; they are the purpose for it.

When alums write, we try to answer soon, and make sure their names are spelled correctly. Our graduates are doing us a good turn when they choose to call; we are not doing them a favor by looking up some lost graduate's address or checking on a date for a reunion. Our alums are a part of the school's mission—they are not outsiders!

Our alums (translate friends) are not cold statistics. They are flesh and blood human beings with feelings and emotions like our own. For example, my brother Tom is a Yale Divinity School alum, and therefore one of my constituents. Thus, I need to indulge or humor him, like any good friend, when his thinking goes awry on such matters as politics, theology, and music.

Do *not* argue or fight with alums. You may discuss an issue, but an unhappy alum is rarely a (happy) donor. Learn to trust them; they will soon trust you in turn. Trust is earned, not given. Remember, the Bible tells us that "God loves a cheerful giver," but our school is willing to accept a gift from a grumpy one as well. However, it is much better if all parties are happy about a gift.

Our alums bring us their needs, their wishes, their hopes, their desires. We should be caring enough and competent enough to figure out how to match their needs with those of the school. A couple of years ago, a wonderful lady (a widow of one of our alums) wanted to do something special in memory of her husband's fiftieth reunion. She asked to talk with us *in person* on Friday afternoon, the day after Thanksgiving. The school is closed that day. No one is around. Everyone is stuffed with turkey. I was to be out of town. At my suggestion, the dean and his gracious wife invited the lady to have tea with them at the dean's residence. It was a caring, concerned act of friendship. The visitor asked about some of the needs of the school. Three days before Christmas, she presented the school with a fully paid endowed chair in pastoral counseling, $750,000. The dean has often remarked it was the most successful tea party he ever attended, almost as dramatic as the Boston tea party. Remember, however, the initial reason was *friendship,* not money.

In dealing with alums as friends, remind yourself to love each one as if there were only one in the world to love. Think of each as a person whom you want to serve, not as a person who will do something for you or the seminary. The more one-to-one relationships (quality and quantity) the chief executive officer and the development director can maintain, the greater your chances are to help others and the more loyal your friends will become.

Graduates who truly care about the learned and learning ministry eventually realize that the *desire to give* is paramount. All else follows from that. The amount is less important than the act of giving.

How to deal with alums? Ralph Waldo Emerson said it well 115 years ago: "It is one of the most beautiful compensations of life that no one can sincerely try to help another without helping himself."

Romancing Alums:
First Meeting Through Retirement

Jewell Perkins Eanes

I am struck by how similar our cultivation of alums is to a romantic relationship. Just as in courtship, we attempt to attract the attention and capture the interest of our students, even prior to graduation. We invest time and energy in complimenting them on their achievements and on their present and future potential. We solicit a commitment to our shared relationship. We stroke them at every opportunity, reminding them of the splendid moments we have shared and of the common bond we hold dear.

Yes, it is a courtship and, yes, we do regard our alums as our significant others. They hold the key to how Garrett-Evangelical is viewed by the church and by the wider world. They also hold the key to the seminary's purse as we count on about forty-four percent of our faithful alums to give each year. We tend this relationship with great care. We are constantly seeking ways to enhance the relationship and to keep it fresh and exciting. We work diligently to maintain open communication that tells our alums how much we care about them and how much we want to continue a blissful future with them.

From the moment that a new student arrives at our institution we consider that student a pre-alum and deserving of our time and attention. This year our first encounter with new students was at registration. We sought a high visibility opportunity and attempted to promote a broad understanding of the integral role the development office plays in the life of the seminary. We staffed a station in the registration process where we served refreshments and showed them we were a warm, friendly, and helpful office.

We also developed a welcome brochure which invited students to help us help them. In the brochure we informed them that the development office is responsible for raising money for student scholarships, library resources, and salaries. We reminded them how important it is to write a personal thank you note to their scholarship donors, and we encouraged their participation in our phonathon. We advertised for part-time help in the development office. Through a tear-out portion of the brochure we invited them to provide the names and addresses of family members and home churches so that we could send them copies of the seminary newsletter.

In seeking opportunities for interaction with our students, we have involved them in our scholarship luncheon and leadership dinner. Each year scholarship donors and student recipients are invited to attend chapel together, followed by a luncheon where they get to know one another personally. Pictures are taken of the donors and recipients and shared with the donors in our follow-up communication. At the leadership dinner we use every opportunity to showcase our students through student panels and musical presentations. Students are also invited to participate on information panels at other functions sponsored by the development office during the year, including President's Weekend (a program for prospective donors), reunion gatherings, and alum board meetings.

At the midpoint of the academic year we begin a more concentrated focus on our graduating seniors. We select a gift chair and assist the chair in organizing a senior gift committee to promote the senior class gift program. With the support and encouragement of the development office, the seniors vote on a class gift. Past gifts have been earmarked for an elevator for the seminary's main building, scholarships, stained glass windows for the chapel, a grand piano, and a student lounge.

The success of the class gift project rests heavily on the enthusiasm and creativity of the student chair and how dedicated the committee is in soliciting the support of classmates. In addition to outright gifts and five-year pledges, students have the rather painless option of earmarking their housing deposits toward the class gift. Other strategies have included inviting parents and home churches to make a gift to the class project in honor of their graduating senior. An honor roll of donors and honorees is then presented at the senior chapel service during commencement activities.

During commencement week each graduate is given a senior packet which contains letters from me and the chair of the alum board welcoming the graduate into the alum association. The graduate also receives an institutional logo pin and a form to complete regarding future plans and a permanent address for alum files.

Approximately one month following commencement, I send a letter of good wishes to our recent graduates and enclose a senior class group picture. Additionally, as the office of seminary relations receives notification from various annual conferences concerning first appointments, a letter of good wishes in this new appointment is sent to the graduate.

Our class steward program is a major way we keep in touch with each of our classes. It is designed to promote giving to current operations by our alums. A class steward from each of the past sixty-seven graduating classes is chosen by our office. We attempt to choose individuals who have demonstrated by their own stewardship an ongoing interest in the seminary. Class stewards encourage their classmates to give by their personal enthusiasm and generous example. Their letters provide a warmth that is impossible to capture in a brochure or form letter because these are letters to classmates, colleagues, friends.

The goals of the class steward program are to encourage current donors to upgrade their gifts and non-donors to make a gift. The class steward's role, however, is not so much to convince a classmate to give as it is to keep that classmate in the habit of giving. While class spirit is sometimes enough to provide incentive for giving, more often the impetus is the seminary itself, and the importance of supporting high quality theological education.

We ask class stewards to serve for a period of at least two years. The seminary provides the class stewards with adequate resources and support. We give them a handbook of information about the seminary and the class steward program, a confidential class list with current data and giving histories, and sample letters. Monthly reports, showing class progress, are mailed to each class steward.

We prefer that class stewards use their own personal church or business letterhead for their correspondence, but we will create a letterhead for them if requested. We give class stewards the option of developing their own letter or revising one of the sample letters. They may print their own letters, after we have edited the copy, or have our office print the letters and send back to them for their signatures. We provide first-class postage to be affixed to envelopes which bear the class steward's return address. We reimburse class stewards for any out-of-pocket expenses, such as telephone and postage expenses, if they request this. Some class stewards donate these expenses to the seminary as part of their annual gift.

Class stewards provide valuable assistance to the seminary, but their role is not without personal benefit. They have the satisfaction of knowing they are influencing the quality of education for future seminarians. They are given an opportunity to build better communication among class members as well as with the seminary itself.

We ask class stewards to commit to a code of ethics. This code of ethics requests that they keep confidential matters confidential, and that they carry out their responsibilities according to the specified standards. We ask that they approach their tasks with enthusiasm and accept training when it is offered. We encourage them to be as creative as possible and to project their own personalities. We encourage them to add hand-written comments to their letters, and even to send Christmas cards.

Some of our class stewards have established such strong communication ties with their classmates that they are reluctant to give up their position. We have to nudge them gently into retirement in order that other persons may inject new enthusiasm into the program.

As the class steward letters start to arrive each fall and winter, I feel blessed to read their reflections on their seminary experiences and to learn of their devotion to the institution. These letters are frequently inspirational and are personal faith statements. Letters written by class stewards who are serving in pastoral ministry give an inside view into the kind of leadership and spiritual direction these graduates provide the parishes they serve. Their letters often serve to recharge my own thinking and to help me tackle my tasks with renewed enthusiasm.

Working with the class stewards and communicating with them monthly allows a friendship to develop that otherwise I would not have the opportunity to experience. In turn, I attempt to make my monthly communications with the class stewards more than simply cover letters for their gift and pledge reports. I update them on happenings at the seminary, send them copies of sermons preached in chapel, and attempt to strengthen their ties to the institution. At the end of the fiscal year, I give them a gift from the seminary, usually a book written by one of our faculty.

Reunions provide another opportunity to romance our alums. Each spring we have a series of lectures the week following Easter. We send an invitation to all alums at the end of January announcing the lectures and inviting them to return to campus. One day of that week is designated as Reunion Day. While all alums are invited to participate in Reunion Day, we especially cultivate those who graduated five, ten, twenty-five, thirty, and forty years ago.

These special classes receive personalized letters referencing their anniversary year. They also receive profile forms which we ask them to complete. These forms include data regarding career, family, special educational achievements, and professional recognitions. We combine these forms into a reunion booklet and distribute them during Reunion Day to those present and mail the remaining booklets to those who could not attend. The booklets also contain a class listing with current addresses to facilitate communication among classmates.

Reunion Day activities include worship, campus tours,

and plenty of time for socializing. The highlight is always the alum banquet. A typical program format for the alum banquet would include a "state of the seminary" report by the president, a keynote speech from one of the faculty, and music by our students. We also choose a class representative from each of the anniversary classes to give a five-minute highlight of their seminary years.

Our fiftieth anniversary reunion is held in connection with commencement in June and is a two-day event. We attempt to whet their appetite for the celebration with monthly mailings to our fifty-year class.

We roll out the red carpet for this golden group. They are the seminary's guests for two nights at a local hotel. When they arrive at the hotel, they find a note of welcome, a copy of the agenda, and a small basket of fruit and snacks. On the first day the guests participate in a welcome reception, lunch, campus tours, and a worship service prepared just for them. That evening they join the faculty, administration, and trustees for dinner and an evening of entertainment. A hospitality room is reserved at the hotel where alums can gather after the dinner and reminisce into the night if they desire.

On the second day the alums are presented with corsages and boutonnieres and escorted to the senior chapel service where they are seated in a reserved section. Following the chapel service, the alums have a golden anniversary luncheon prior to the afternoon commencement ceremonies.

At commencement the alums are again seated in a reserved section of the sanctuary. Early in the service they are escorted to the platform where they are individually introduced, and the president reads a brief biographical sketch telling of each alum's life.

The fifty-year alums conclude their reunion by joining in the post commencement reception. By this time they are aglow with wonderful memories and happy with the recognition and tender care they have received. Along with many nice thank you letters have come several nice gifts.

One of the newest alum recognition methods we use is honoring alums on their birthdays. We have added birth dates to our data bank, and we now send birthday cards to all alums for whom we have birth dates. Monthly listings of the birthdays are also placed in the chapel and alums are remembered in prayer during the month of their birth. A member of our support staff suggested this plan and has taken the responsibility of hand addressing these cards each month and preparing the list for the chapel. Our alums have embraced this recognition with much warmth, and we regularly receive letters from them thanking us for remembering their birthdays.

Each year, through an all-alum mailing, we invite alums to submit nominations for persons they believe to be deserving of special recognition by the seminary. These nominations, along with supporting data, are given to the executive committee of the alum board for final selections. Usually two alums are selected: one with twenty-five years or more in ministry, and one with less than twenty-five years in ministry. The distinguished alums are honored at the commencement ceremony and given a distinguished service plaque. The honorees are also invited to speak briefly at the commencement service.

I tend to view our alums as our stockholders. When they are happy, I rejoice with them. When they are displeased with some aspect of the seminary, I work to restore their confidence. When our alums make suggestions, I believe their suggestions, whatever they are, are intended to enhance the seminary and I treat their suggestions with respect. I never forget that our alums are persons who have given their lives to the service of others. Working with them is a privilege, and I hold them in great esteem.

You and I have been given the awesome responsibility of searching for those who "live to give" and for those who are on fire to help others. It is an exciting task. I wish you courage when the search is difficult. I wish you joy for the successes—and the successes will come. And I invite you to embrace the task with passion, for it will make all the difference for you and for your institution.

Ten Commandments for a Successful Class Agent Program

David Heetland

How would you like to raise significantly more dollars for current operations from your alums? That's what Garrett-Evangelical Theological Seminary did in the first year of its class agent program, with no additional staff and a very modest budget. Here are its ten commandments for starting a successful class agent program:

1. Make the class agent program a priority. We had talked about beginning such a program for a long time. It didn't actually happen, however, until we made it a priority and wrote it into our development action plan.

2. Research what other institutions have done. We collected materials from other institutions that have class agent programs and talked to the persons in charge of these programs. They helped us avoid pitfalls and pointed out what worked well for them. We then designed our own program utilizing key insights from several other established and successful programs.

3. Recruit your class agents. This is the most important, and the most difficult, part of the process. We decided to recruit class agents from the past sixty-seven graduating classes. We reviewed class lists, identified top givers, and issued invitations. Twenty-five percent responded positively to these invitations. The rest were recruited by phone. In the phone call the class agent program was explained and their assistance was invited. Eventually sixty-seven willing workers were found.

4. Provide a job description. Our job description was quite simple. Each class agent was expected to send two letters to class members: one in the fall and another in the spring to those who had not yet responded. In addition, agents were encouraged to assist in the fiscal year wrap-up.

5. Set goals for each class. We reviewed the previous year's giving history to determine the number of persons contributing in each class and the dollars contributed. Participation and dollar goals were then established. Each class was challenged to surpass previous giving/participation levels, and reunion classes were given special (translate "even higher") goals.

6. Offer to assist. We tried to assist the class agents in whatever way possible so they would be successful. We provided sample letters that they could use if they wanted. Some used them verbatim. Others tossed them out and started all over—in some remarkably creative ways. While we encouraged them to use their own stationery, we offered to prepare their letters for them if they needed, and we even ended up preparing stationery for several. Postage was provided, and agents were assured that we were only a phone call away.

7. Monitor progress and keep agents informed. Agents were instructed to send us a copy of the letter at the same time it went to their classmates, so we could monitor when they actually went out. Our office, in turn, sent agents monthly updates on pledges and gifts received, so they knew where they stood in relation to their goals.

8. Work on wrap-up. As we neared the end of the fiscal year, we encouraged agents to make a final effort to contact with a phone call or a personal note those class members who had made no response. Again we offered to provide the notecards and reimburse them for the phone calls. Twenty-six of the sixty-seven class agents assisted in this wrap-up.

9. Express appreciation. We told our class agents thanks in several ways: with letters, phone calls, and gifts (seminary tee shirts). We also provided a list of class agents to our trustees and encouraged them to express thanks to any they personally knew.

10. Begin planning immediately for another year. As soon as the fiscal year was over we began recruiting class agents once again. We only had to recruit nineteen this year, however, as the rest have agreed to serve another year. This year we have also prepared a class agent manual which includes a detailed timeline, tips on writing good letters, and even examples of last year's creative masterpieces! We anticipate that the second year will be easier, and we hope just as successful.

And how successful was their first year? Forty of the sixty-seven classes showed an increase in dollar support. A total of $25,042 more than the previous year was received from alums for current operations, for a grand total of $130,726.

Thirty-five of the sixty-seven classes showed an increase in the number of persons participating. Over a hundred more alums contributed to current operations than the previous year, with a total alum participation rate of forty-two percent.

The cost for the first year of this program was approximately $3,000, or twelve cents for each new dollar raised, well under the average educational institution cost of sixteen cents to raise a dollar.

There you have it—ten commandments for starting a successful class agent program. May you be blessed with similar results!

Prospect Research on the Run

James M. Wray, Jr.

Prospect research is a challenge in the small shop development office. Though staff and resources are limited, research must be done for a viable development program. How does one gather the information needed to cultivate donors for the next gift and bring new donors into the circle of friends who support our institution? Following are some sources that have been helpful for doing prospect research "on the run."

Church newsletters. Select newsletters from churches that are most significant to the institution. Scan them for new information about donors and information that may suggest prospective donors. Notices about deaths, promotions, and transfers, as well as announcements of people elected to church offices, can be significant.

Newspapers. The business section of newspapers can contain information that helps fill in the profile of a donor or prospective donor.

Civic and cultural events. The printed program distributed at civic and cultural events often recognizes individuals and businesses whose gifts have made the event possible. This data can be informative about current donors and suggest new ones.

Trustees. Trustees may have access to business and financial data through a computerized data bank service or through specialized printed resources. Trustees may be willing to secure information on specific individuals or businesses. Trustees in business, law, finance, and insurance frequently know or can get information necessary in completing a prospective donor profile. Ask!

Ministers. Ministers, and particularly ministers who are alums, are one of the most helpful resources. They provide names when asked, "Who in your congregation can help the seminary?"

They will also give specific information about individuals when asked. The ministers must trust the development officer to treat the information confidentially and respect the person on whom the information is given. Keep the minister informed about cultivation and solicitation of the prospective donor. A well-informed minister is a valuable ally.

Universities. The small shop seminary development office does not have the budget to purchase many of the useful research tools that may be found in a large university's development office. If you are near such a university, inquire as to whether or not you are welcome to use the university's resources.

Development secretary. The secretary usually handles gifts and address changes. The secretary can watch for an increase in the size of a gift, a check written on a business account, an increase in the frequency of giving, and changes in names and addresses. Encourage the secretary to be attentive to such information.

Donors. Individuals who support the institution know many people who have interests and incomes similar to theirs. Opportunities for donors to suggest prospective donors should be presented. This can be achieved during a personal visit with a donor or with a response form included in a direct mail piece.

Faculty. A seminary's faculty members are frequently engaged in lecturing and preaching in congregations, and leading workshops, retreats, seminars and conferences for churches. Educate the faculty to recognize opportunities for prospect identification, research, and cultivation in these settings.

Students. Many seminarians serve churches while in seminary. Many have strong ties to their home congregation. Introducing students to the work of the development office and giving them opportunity to suggest potential donors can be beneficial.

When asking another person to suggest prospective donors, give the person some categories to guide their thinking. It is also instructive for development officers to be attentive to certain conditions in the lives of persons, such as the following:

a couple with no children,

a widow or widower without children,

single or married elderly whose children have "made it,"

person of obvious wealth,

person who owns much real estate,

person who has been in the stock market for several years,

person who anticipates selling or has recently sold a business,

person who has received an inheritance,

person who has a life-changing experience,

person who fits one of the above categories and demonstrates commitment to the church.

People with whom we work in prospect research probably have in the back of their minds, or on the tip of their tongues, the question, "What will this development officer do with the information being requested from me?" Be forthright in discussing how the information will be used and honor how the people providing the information prefer the information to be handled. Thanking the people for their important contribution, and informing them when their information leads ultimately to a gift, will assure the development office of a nucleus of committed friends.

On the Road Again:
Making the Most Out of
Development Travel

Wesley F. Brown

In Lewis Carroll's classic story, *Alice in Wonderland,* there is a scene in the forest where Alice, quite bewildered, asks the Cheshire Cat for directions. When the Cat ascertains that she has no particular destination, he observes that if you don't know where you're going, any road will get you there.

For the development officer, expectations meet reality in the routine experiences of prospect and donor visitation. The thoughtful preparation and execution of plans, with a clear understanding of the preferred destination, is essential. Here then are some observations and suggestions, perhaps most useful to individuals new in the field, for making the most out of travel for development.

Know the seminary. An institutional plan—owned by the board, staff, faculty, students, alums—is a prerequisite. Going on the road without an institutional plan is like traveling alone in a faraway country without signs or road maps. Potential donors want to be involved with a seminary that knows its mission and how it may be achieved.

Know yourself. The integrity and credibility of the development officer cannot be overstated. You need to be able to speak decisively for the seminary while also understanding the boundaries of your own authority. Every development contact either enhances the mission or detracts from it.

Know the individuals you plan to visit. Be certain that they know you, even if you have only met over the telephone. Keep prospect files current. With every prospect or donor, the more complete the file—on family, interests, church and institutional relationships, volunteer service, personal resources, and other philanthropy—the more informed and appropriate the approach and the more likely the success.

Maintain a priority visitation list. Prioritize by geographical area your top thirty (or a number appropriate for the size of the staff) donor prospects for the institution. This is essential not only for the development officer who plans a series of visits but also for the key administrator, faculty member, or staff person who may, while in a city on other business, be able, with the right information, to make a useful development call on behalf of the seminary.

Visit and thank selected previous major givers. They will likely continue to give—perhaps at increased levels—provided that you keep them informed and maintain a relationship based upon trust and institutional integrity.

Schedule the CEO. Take the president or dean literally when he or she says, "Go ahead, make my day." Scheduling the chief executive officer to the critical calls is an important dimension of the development task and it should be done routinely.

Plan visits for the best time. Florida is too hot in the summer. No one wants to visit with a development officer the day after Thanksgiving or on April 15. Know how recently contact has been made with the donor through a previous visit, telephone call, or letter. It is not helpful to knock on the door too often but several years between visits guarantees the out-of-sight, out-of-mind attitude and essentially negates earlier cultivation.

Schedule carefully. Write several weeks ahead, indicating that you plan to be in the area, would like to see the prospect, and will call to make arrangements. A subsequent telephone call sets the time and place. A brief note reconfirms the plan.

Do not over-schedule. Trying to make too many calls in a day leads to rushed visits, unforgivable tardiness, and inevitable frustration. It is often difficult to anticipate the time and distance between appointment number one and appointment number two. Take prospects out to breakfast, lunch, or dinner.

Visit alums. While they tend not to be prospects for major financial contributions, their advice is a considerable contribution in itself. As with any gift, though, you usually have to ask for it. Visits on the road with graduates in a particular region, individually or in a group setting, can provide the chance to ask about specific prospects, donors, or foundations. A brief meeting reaffirms ties with the seminary and provides an opportunity to thank the alums for their support.

Ask for leads from former congregations. Rarely will pastors provide names from their current congregation, but they are much more inclined to tell you about people from their former churches. How might they be cultivated? Who could consider endowing a scholarship to honor her pastor? Who needs to have his sights raised?

Listen carefully. Encourage conversation about what the prospect wishes to accomplish and how. You are a guest, a personification of the seminary. The prospect is under no obligation to become a major donor. Be ready for surprises, including happy ones. If the anticipated direction of interest and action is not right, have alternatives in minds. Make notes immediately after the visit. It is amazing how quickly details can be lost, especially if several calls are scheduled in rapid succession.

Follow up promptly. A letter of thanks is also the best occasion for summarizing what was said and reinforcing what was agreed upon, including the subsequent actions to be taken: What questions can be answered? Will a proposal be presented? When will we need to meet again? Effective development work depends fundamentally upon careful attention to details.

Be a good steward of institutional resources. A great deal of money may be spent quickly and unnecessarily when traveling. Planning ahead saves money. Keep a current road atlas, regional maps from rental car agencies, and national hotel/motel directories on file in the development office. Join the frequent flyer and preferred guest club programs and secure the services of a competent travel agent. Evaluate time involved so that, between too much travel and too little, a good balance may be achieved.

Travel for seminary development is exhilarating, exhausting, and essential. Professional fund raisers, just as professional athletes, must invest a great deal of time and energy in "road work" because positive results are impossible without disciplined preparation.

For all who are going out once again, with plans carefully made and the destination clearly understood, in the words of the ancient Irish blessing, "May the road rise to meet you . . . and may the Lord hold you in the palm of his hand."

Involving Friends
in the Life of Your School

Royal A. Govain

More than ninety percent of our fund raising support at Harvard comes from friends of the Divinity School. We define friends as individuals who are not graduates of the school. By and large they have had no theological education. We believe that our greatest potential for future support rests with this group. Consequently we spend the largest portion of our resources developing programs to attract friends to the school and to maintain their involvement and gift support.

At first glance this would seem to be an especially difficult task. Theological education is largely unknown to today's educated population. Many see it as "shrouded in vestments" and "clouded in incense." At best it is misunderstood.

However, upon further reflection on the enterprise of theology, this task is made much easier. Theology pervades so many fields that it is not difficult at all to think about "interest clusters" that can serve as doorways into what we do in seminaries and divinity schools. For example, the environment, public policy, medicine, the law, international relations, world history, archaeology—all are subjects that attract interest from groups of people in the general population who may or may not identify themselves as "religious." In fact, we should be aware that some potential friends clearly do not perceive themselves as "religious," yet they hold strong personal convictions in accord with our goals.

A careful examination of your school's programs can uncover the list of potential friends and set the framework for your strategy to enlist their "friendship." Below are some steps that we have used and have found to be successful:

Inventory your current theological resources for their

interconnections to other fields. Do you have special programs that relate to values, science, and technology; the environment; public policy development; Biblical archaeology; public health delivery; world religions and politics; the church and the urban underclass? Do you have particular faculty experts who are resources on various subjects of current regional, national, or world interest?

Develop a list of attributes of potential friends. With your inventory and a broader perspective on your school's theological education, develop a list of the kinds of characteristics and attributes potential friends are likely to have. These might include involvement in and support of nonprofit organizations and movements, professional and/or business affiliations with related issues, and personal or family history shaped by various religious/societal forces in which you have expertise. Keep in mind, of course, that the capability to make substantial gifts to your school must be the common denominator.

Review the attributes list with alum leaders and trustees. Ask your alums and trustees to help you identify both individuals who have these attributes and groups with whom mutual interests exist. For example, international human development agencies, community organizations, health and social service movements—all are involved in activities complementary to our mission of theological education. Use this task as a means of developing within your current volunteer leadership an ongoing broader concept of the reach of your theological education into other academic and professional disciplines, and therefore the potential for attracting a greatly expanded constituency.

Review your students' backgrounds. Look over the educational and prior professional backgrounds of your students. Many of them will have experience that will resonate well with groups of potential friends. Their stories about why they are seeking a theological education will often be most articulate. Ask them to talk about how theology is informing and enhancing their understanding of medicine, law, business, or public policy, and deliver their messages to the various appropriate constituency groups.

Sponsor topical conferences. Combine your inventory, the attributes of potential friends, and your students' backgrounds to determine a series of interdisciplinary conferences on specific topics of public concern you could sponsor, or better still, jointly sponsor with other groups and organizations. The goal is to bring together your faculty and students with experts and supporters of other areas.

View this as an opportunity to expose lay people to theological education and to the resources of theology that can substantively contribute to other fields and disciplines. As an example, a few months after the presidential campaign, we co-sponsored a conference with the John F. Kennedy School of Government at Harvard on "Values and Images in Presidential Politics." The conference brought journalists, public policy scholars, theologians, elected officials, and interested friends together. We have jointly sponsored similar meetings with other groups that focused on the environment, media coverage of the holocaust, and reproductive technologies.

Determine other avenues for outside involvement. Welcome the involvement and input from individuals and groups from outside the theological world. Invite individuals to attend special programs, lectures, and other activities; that is to say, cultivate their interest. Solicit their service on various ad hoc and standing committees and task forces. Whenever we have an outside lecturer, we develop a small list of friends who might be interested and we issue them a personal invitation. We have individuals who are not graduates of the school in all major leadership positions and advisory councils (with the exception of the alum council).

Educate friends on the components of theological education. Use every opportunity to educate your friends on how their interests have a context within all the components of theological education. We always outline how a particular special project or program contributes to our overall efforts within the curriculum or to the broad educational environment we foster.

We try to demonstrate how all our activities are directed toward our mission.

Communicate funding needs for special interest projects. Seek initial small support for special projects that most closely match the interests of specific friends. Provide superb stewardship on those initial gifts. This will build donor confidence in your school's management of its contributions and will enable you to articulate more effectively your broader needs. Several of our initial gifts from friends were special grants for conferences such as those noted above.

Cultivate and solicit major gifts. Eventually (sometimes even rather quickly) you will find that you are in a position to discuss the major needs of your school and to solicit a gift from a friend. At the outset, he or she may not have understood that the components of the mission of theological education were congruent with any personal interests, but your friend will now find himself or herself considering a major gift to the school.

Ask friends to identify other potential friends. Always ask your school's friends to keep the school in mind when talking to others. "Converts" are often the best spokespersons for approaches to other potential friends.

Remember that our role in development is educating about theological education. The vitality of the theological education our schools offer is dependent upon outside support and upon the communication that theology can foster among and between disciplines. The involvement of friends in our schools is critical to this process.

Donor Cultivation

M. Katherine Welles-Snyder

Development is becoming increasingly competitive nationwide. Old funding resources are drying up. In many cases our constituents are aging and on fixed incomes. We are graduating fewer students. The recession has affected individual and church support. What do we do now?

As development professionals, we need to look for new prospects, in new places, and learn new ways of cultivation. To do this, we first need to know exactly who our constituents are: trustees, friends, alums. Next, we need to be familiar with the profile of our current constituency: age, profession, interests, faith commitment. Then we need to ask ourselves: How can we alter this profile and find new sources of support? Whom can we reach out to in addition to these groups?

Another important step in developing new constituents is to dispel old myths. For some time I labored under the misguided assumption that the wealthy were always the typical "corporate type." Then I read about a small business owner who gave $100 million to a local community college. Clearly, I was not looking in the right place. We need to look at different sources, such as women, minorities, ethnic groups, and persons with inherited wealth, and we must learn how to cultivate and solicit these groups.

Cultivation, as defined by Webster's New World Dictionary, is the process of giving attention to the development, growth, or improvement of something. Webster also defines *relationship* as the process of building connections between or among people, institutions, or nations. Webster's definitions imply that to develop a relationship is to grow connections, to join together two or more entities.

Cultivation for a development officer is the bringing

together of the institution and the individual. It is a process of joining and strengthening connections. It is a process of initiation by the institution and response from the individual. As the connections strengthen, the institution becomes increasingly important to the individual; it becomes a way of life, part of his or her identity.

Many articles and books have been written on donor cultivation including those by Jerold Panas, M. Jane Williams, and Dave Dunlop. All have made a large contribution to my knowledge and understanding of major gifts and donor cultivation, but none has given me a means to measure the progress of our institution's relationship with an individual. For this I use a "cultivation hierarchy."

The idea of a cultivation hierarchy is probably not new, but defining and applying it has helped me see the process more clearly. Using the multiple of four, I have been able to see the magnitude of our work in terms of desired results. To the uninitiated, the formula is staggering: for every ultimate gift received, we must begin by making 4,096 people aware of our institution and its mission.

As I look at an individual we are cultivating, I try to place that person on the cultivation hierarchy. It helps me to think of it as a pyramid which serves as a kind of map. It helps to determine the stage of the relationship, and the next objective. In this way it provides a basis for strategizing moves to reach the next level.

Awareness. The first step in cultivation is to make the public aware of the institution and its mission. This is done through a well-developed, comprehensive advertisement and public relations campaign. The campaign can be aimed at both general and specific audiences. It might include radio, bus cards, billboards, traveling exhibits, church bulletin inserts (with timely reflections by faculty), ads in weekly newspapers (targeted for specifically defined audiences), and monthly news releases to local and national TV and print media.

Interest. Once awareness is reached, we need to provoke interest. This helps create within the individual a desire to know more about the mission of the institution and a feeling that knowing more would be of personal value. There are several ways to create interest. A quarterly magazine which covers seminary news but also contains some thought provoking and educational articles can create interest, as can a speaker's bureau, film/discussion series, special luncheons hosted by trustees for people they know, educational programs for the public, and sacred music/gospel music concerts.

Involvement. Once interest is there, we must get the individual involved. Involvement is key to the cultivation process. Telling individuals about the mission of the institution is very different from giving them the opportunity to guide, support, and shape the institution. Involving people in the organization will sustain their interest. Without involvement they will quickly lose interest and move on to other organizations which make them feel useful, important, and valued.

Finding ways to involve a large number of people and manage their involvement is not easy. Fortunately, not everyone has the same talents or interests. This helps to divide the responsibility for involvement among various faculty and staff members.

The ways to involve people are varied: a public policy breakfast group (monthly), an executive women's discussion/study group (quarterly), national board (annually), corporators (regional leaders who work on special projects or who sit on board sub-committees), associates (younger people who will become future leaders), and of course the fund raising campaign.

One way to sustain involvement is to help those you are cultivating to bond not just to the institution but to each other. This is important and needs to begin early in the cultivation process. It is the development officer's responsibility to create an environment conducive to bonding. Working groups and social events provide such an opportunity.

Knowledge. Once the individual is involved, it is crucial to transform the involvement into an internalized, personal commitment. Before the individual can internalize the commitment, he or she must have a thorough knowledge of the institution. General knowledge of the institution can be gained by reading the history of the institution, attending classes, chairing a committee, or being a member of a program advisory group.

It is insider knowledge, however, that really solidifies the relationship. To gain real commitment and even love of the institution, we need to strengthen the bond between individual and institution by establishing a level of trust through the knowledge we share. Providing "insider information" demonstrates trust. This can be achieved in one of several ways: through a special insider newsletter which is sent by the president when appropriate, through small intimate dinner parties at the president's home, or through working with the faculty on advisory groups.

Commitment. Few people will reach the commitment stage, but those who do play a key role in the life of the institution.

Those who are committed identify with the goals and mission of the institution which they help shape. Individuals who are committed to the institution share its beliefs and values. The individual's relationship with the institution is much like family, and at this stage of cultivation recognition of the individual's contributions to the institutional community is very important.

Love. Developing love for an institution takes time and is developed, I believe, much like the love for a friend. It involves trust, shared experiences and knowledge, shared goals, shared vision, and an unselfish willingness by both the institution and individual to do whatever each can for the other. Love is a give-and-take relationship. It must be consummated by recognizing and publicly demonstrating the value of the relationship—individual to the institution and institution to the individual.

Cultivation is a never-ending cycle of information gathering and relationship building, but if we concentrate on developing strong relationships with individuals, the dollars will follow. The cultivation process is something which demands strict personal discipline on the part of the development officer. A formal process to identify prospects, develop and review strategies, and track/follow up on moves is essential.

For me, donor cultivation is twenty-five percent art, twenty-five percent science, fifty percent strategy, and two hundred percent hard work. But if done well, it pays off.

Raising Support
from the Local Church

Douglas H. Scott

At the two seminaries I have served, local church support provides thirty-five to forty-five percent of the annual fund. Yet, raising support from churches is a long, hard process, and can be very frustrating.

As a young, energetic director of church relations, I spent the first two years of my development career raising church support "by osmosis." I visited hundreds of pastors, thanked each one for the support given by the church, timidly asked for an increase in next year's budget and moved on to my next appointment. By the time the annual mission budget was being constructed, the pastor had no doubt forgotten my visit. If by chance the pastor did remember, it was still unlikely that the message was delivered. After all, it was possibly months since my visit. So we got what we deserved—little or no increase.

There just had to be a better, more effective way. How could I raise the giving levels of local congregations? How could I tell the story to local churches? How could I encourage ownership of the seminary by the local church? How could I maintain control of my own success rather than leave it in the hands of a well-intentioned pastor, who may or may not have it as a priority?

I started by building a strategy based on some of the same principles we all use with major gift donors and major gift prospects. The outcome is basically a five step process.

1. Identify and target top prospect churches. At Central Seminary we have 750 local churches in our denominational designated support area. There is no way to work effectively with that number, at least not with a staff of two. Since the churches are located in places between Missouri and Colorado, North

Dakota and Texas, we can't even think about visiting everyone. Thirty to forty key churches seems like a manageable number. We target based on size, mission budget, total budget, and previous giving. We don't ignore non-targeted churches. We visit when a representative is in the area. Each non-targeted church also receives written requests for annual fund support, plus other public relations materials.

2. Make a personal visit with the pastor and/or pastoral staff. This is a key step. My agenda is four-fold. First, it is to gain the respect of the pastor. Second, it is to make the pastor my partner in presenting the needs of the seminary to the appropriate board and eventually to the congregation. Third, I want the pastor to tell me what the church "could do" (not "would do") if properly motivated. How do I get that information? I ask. Finally, I want the pastor to invite me to send a written proposal outlining the seminary needs and asking the church to provide for those needs. (Yes, I ask for the invite. I've never been told no.)

3. Prepare and send a written proposal. We do proposals for foundations, corporations, major gift donors, and prospects. Why not churches? We use a straight-forward, five-page, three-part proposal tailored for each of our target churches. Part one outlines the seminary's needs and dependence on annual fund church support. The second part is our ask. We ask for a specific amount, usually what the pastor has already agreed the church "could do" if motivated. Part three outlines the seminary's resources that are available to undergird and enhance the local church's ministries; i.e., what the church is getting for its gift support.

There are several advantages to a written proposal:

The pastor doesn't have to represent the seminary to the mission board. Copies can be prepared for each board member.

You retain control of telling your story the way it needs to be told. It's in the proposal.

The mission board is challenged to consider a specific giving level, probably within its capability since the pastor suggested it.

It looks well-prepared and impressive.

I know of at least one church where we received the entire increase in annual mission giving. We asked the church to double its support from $3,500 to $7,000 a year. The normal practice of this church was to provide five percent across-the-board increases, based on a $70,000 mission budget. Our five percent share would have been $175. When I inquired why we were so lucky, it was simply stated that we asked and nobody else did.

Proposals are flexible. We use them with churches where significant increases are being sought. We also tailor proposals to encourage churches to start new support of the seminary. More recently, we have tried three- and five-year proposals. Here we have encouraged key churches to commit to a substantially higher level of support over a period of years. This keeps a mission committee focused on the seminary.

4. Follow up on the proposal. Along with the written proposal, we offer to have a seminary representative personally meet with the mission committee at the time of consideration. Our experience indicates that only four to five churches a year actually take us up on the offer. Use of a speaker phone can often provide a presence with the committee without the travel.

Other normal follow-up includes a phone call to the pastor to remind him or her to present the proposal and to answer any questions.

5. Follow up on the congregational decision. We schedule a phone call to the pastor after the congregational vote on a new budget has been completed. We heap tons of praise if all or a portion of our request has been approved. We say we understand if not, but reserve the right to ask again next year.

Does it work? For the past eight years the two seminaries I have worked for have experienced increases ranging from ten to fifteen percent in annual local church support.

Gift Clubs: To Have or Have Not?
or
Oh, The Bodacity of it All

Fred W. Cassell

Bodacious adj. Slang. Intrepidly bold or daring. (Webster, 3rd)

Being a bit bodacious in fund raising is probably a good thing. But there is nothing very bodacious about gift clubs as part of an overall development program. Nearly every eleemosynary institution you can name uses them. They seem a tried and true method of raising funds.

Why then has Princeton Seminary not employed gift clubs up until now, and why is that policy about to change? Those questions are the focus of this article.

One reason we have not used them stems from an old law of physics. Inertia applies as much to the fund raising field as to the physical world. An object at rest tends to stay at rest, and an object in motion tends to continue moving in the same direction, unless acted on by some outside force. So we don't have gift clubs partly because we have never had them.

That is not the whole story, of course, because we have thought about, talked about, even argued about it with a consultant who wanted us to start gift clubs several years ago. So it is not just sloth on our part, or the want of the idea, that has kept us from establishing gift clubs. We had a reason, one that will continue to keep us from using gift clubs with our alums. Every time we have asked our class stewards (representatives who head up the fund raising in their respective classes) whether or not to begin gift clubs, they have said to us rather emphatically, "Don't do it! They smack of competition, not cooperation. They pit haves against have-nots. They are the antithesis of Jesus' praising of the widow's two copper coins. They seem to imply that those who are able to give large gifts are more valued by the institution than those who are only able to give small ones. Is not the pastor in a tiny parish living on minimum salary who gives a modest gift to be recognized equally for his/her loyalty to the institution with the pastor of a tall steeple congregation whose salary may be six figures?" And the capper of the argument always goes something like, "Is it Christian (ouch!) to make these kinds of distinctions among those who seek to support the mission of a theological institution? What theological justification can be made to support this practice? Huh?!"

And so we have not started them. God knows we want our fund raising to be theologically correct (TC) even if our language is not always politically correct (PC)!

That argument continues to be persuasive where our alums are concerned. We know it would offend some—maybe many—and we feel it would not be worth doing, even if we could square it with our theology.

But what about our non-alum friends of the institution? They are accustomed to being placed in giving categories by other charitable institutions, and there is no indication that they are offended by seeing their names in one gift club while their friends' and neighbors' names are listed in another. Why not have gift clubs for them?

Now, let me sort out what is beginning to appear to many of you as an obvious contradiction. If it is "theologically insupportable" to have gift clubs, or even "unchristian," then isn't it as wrong to have them for nonalums as for alums? The answer is, of course, yes. But I did not say I (or we in the development department, or the members of the trustees' committee which oversees our development program) consider it unchristian or inappropriate. I said some of our alums feel that way and we do not want to disturb their sensibilities, or (to put it positively) we want to honor their feelings and beliefs.

I personally do not think there is anything wrong with a

little healthy competition, or with raising the sights of folks as encouragement to stretch. "A (person's) reach should exceed (his/her) grasp, or what's a heaven for?" said Robert Browning. My college swimming coach taught me a lesson more than forty years ago that I have not forgotten. Talking together as coach and captain of the team, he and I got into a little philosophical discussion about athletics and I made the mistake of quoting Grantland Rice to him: It is "not that you won or lost, but how you played the game." My coach looked me square in the eye and said, "Listen, Fred, there is only one reason they keep score!"

A little friendly competition never hurt anybody. Of course, competition can get out of hand and no longer be friendly. Then it does hurt people. When winning becomes, in Vince Lombardi's words, not simply a good thing, but "the only thing," then a corner has been turned. But that is a whole different article. What is relevant here is that we (the development department) are not offended by gift clubs, and what is perhaps even more to the point, our trustees are not offended by them. In fact, it was a minister trustee who recently raised the question with me that has led us to do what we are going to do: begin segmenting our non-alum donors into various gift clubs. We are beginning that practice with the unanimous encouragement of our trustees.

Why consider this practice? For one thing I am impressed by the example set by so many other organizations and institutions. Since many of them have been in the fund raising business a lot longer than I have, I have to ask, "Do they know something I don't?" My conclusion is that they probably do.

Also, I think everybody needs some goal to shoot for, some standard by which to judge their performances, some criteria by which to measure what they do. I know I do. When I noticed a couple of years ago that giving fifty bucks more a year to my college would move me into another club, I wrote a bigger check. No big deal. No pressure to do it. No appeals to competition. No promises of glory for increasing my gift. No whistles, hats, or horns when I did. Just my name listed in The Blue and White Club instead of The Founder's Club when the next year's annual report was published. The mere existence of gift clubs accomplished its purpose with me.

We all want people to give more. Isn't that what fund raising is all about? Getting people to give, and then getting them to give more in support of a good and worthy cause. In our case (yours and mine), the cause is theological education in general, and our specific institution in particular. If we want people to give and to raise their levels of giving, why not give them something specific at which to aim?

And so we are going to institute gift clubs for our non-alum friends. The levels of giving have been pegged at places where we have found natural dividing lines: $100, $250, $500, $1,000, $2,500, and $5,000. As of this writing we are still wrestling with appropriate names for these various levels. Not that we think a rose by some other name will smell any sweeter, but hey, you have to have something to wrestle with, right?

Two names suggested for the $0-99 donor club have been The Skinflints and the Pinch Pennies. We have rejected both. I said we fund raisers needed to be a little bodacious, not stupid!

A Critique of Seminary Publications

Celia Luxmoore

A great deal of time, effort, and money is dedicated by seminaries to printed materials. It is important that this investment reflect the style and image of the institution and convey some excitement about events on campus.

Some schools believe in an individual style, well-written and tightly edited, with good photographs, and carried through as a related series of pieces by a professional designer. Unfortunately, too many seminary publications are dull, sparkless, lacking in individuality, and old-fashioned in appearance.

Whether or not the seminary is yet ready to use the word "marketing" openly, publications are the marketing message to various audiences. The messages sent must spring from the school's mission statement, objectives, and strategic plan. Publications are directed to those goals and are part of the image of the seminary conveyed to prospective students, alums, faculty, trustees, continuing education users, donors, and others. From this base of the school's objectives, a marketing plan should be formed to "sell the seminary" to gain both students and gift income.

Philip Kotler, an author on nonprofit marketing, defines marketing as *"the analysis, planning, implementation, and control of carefully formulated programs designed to bring about voluntary exchanges of values with target markets for the purpose of achieving organizational objectives."*

Working in the three markets—education, church denomination, and donor—seminaries need to address these questions: What is our marketing mission as defined by the school's mission statement? Who are our target markets? Prospective students? Donors? What is our institutional image? Traditional? Contemporary? Innovative? How does our seminary differ from others? Where are we positioned in the market against the competition? What themes and messages do we want to send? What are our measurable goals?

Audiences. For each audience we must ask: Who are they? Are they changing? What is the audience's image of the seminary? Is the audience satisfied with the institution? Are there mindsets against us? Is the institution responsive to comments? What is the seminary's image of itself?

Out of this research should come an institutional marketing plan which provides a road map of future expectations for messages so that everyone in the school understands, interprets, and executes the marketing plan. It also gives an official means to say "No" if the question, "Do you need this publication?" is not satisfactorily answered.

Why this publication? Gain satisfactory answers to these questions before the school publishes anything: Does the activity fit in with our mission and strategic plan? Does the piece fit our marketing plan? Who is the audience? Is it really needed? Does it overlap/duplicate or could it be incorporated in something we have already? Is there money in the departmental budget? Is there a better way (than a printed piece) to communicate to this audience? Person-to-person, personal letter, phone call, direct mail? Move ahead only when you are convinced.

Publication production. Start with these questions:

Who is the audience? Where is geographical concentration? Do they know the seminary? Do they know the city? What age is the audience? What is their lifestyle and social class? For example, major donors are likely to have different expectations than prospective students.

What is the focus? Annual fund or lay education?

Where is your institution? Few are set in context.

When is the start date? Or deadline for admission?

How? Make it easy to respond with a form or envelopes.

Content check list. What is the focus? Is it focused? Is it appropriate to the audience? Does it inform? Does it answer who, why, what, where, when, and how? Is it logical and understandable? Is it the right length? Does it have a selling message on the cover? Does it relate benefits for the audience? Does it inspire action? What is the distribution? Will it reach the right audience? Avoid jargon and edit tightly.

Appearance check list. Does the piece "look" like the seminary? Does it fit in with other pieces? Does the look fit the budget available? Is the size suitable for the method of distribution? Is it readable? Make sure the type is large enough. Paper? Colors? Photographs (stock or special shoot)? Reply cards? Tear offs? Return envelopes?

Design check list. Look at a lot of portfolios to find a designer who will work well with you and has sensitivity to theological education. A good designer has technical knowledge and creative talent which is likely to far exceed your own and is well worth the fee.

Give some direction, but let the designer create. See a rough concept and adjust where necessary to suit the institution or to improve communication. Make sure you or the designer controls the printing process for first-class results.

Things to do. Set a narrow line. For easier reading use wide margins; lay out in blocks or two columns; use more white space, design elements, photographs.

Use larger type. Give readers easy-to-read sizes with space between lines to help readability.

Simplify layout. Make sure headings are hierarchical and size them according to order of importance. Leave space between sections.

Look up-to-date. Keep an eye on trends in slick magazines and copy them.

Use upper- and lower-case type for text. All capitals are hard to read.

Keep type clean. Avoid mixing typefaces, or typewriter face with typeface; underlining bold face is superfluous.

Keep layout clean. Fewer words, fewer elements help readability and attractiveness; try putting complex information in a table.

Keep design simple. Design boldly, but not fussily. Use only one desktop layout gimmick at a time.

Use professional photographs of everybody and everything. Crop them tightly to avoid distraction. Avoid grip-and-grin if you can. Try to catch real interaction.

Run the best photographs large. Avoid running lots of little ones just because they were taken.

Make the cover or front page eye-catching.

Use professional design for a high standard result.

Make sure the half-tones will reproduce the photographs well.

Use a first-class printer and check the press run.

Publications take time and money. Let's continue to reassess the impact of that effort, and direct sufficient funds to make the investment effective for advancing the institution.

Ten Ways to Thank Your Donors

Larry Van Dyke

Can there be anything more enjoyable for the development officer than the opportunity to say "thank you" to your donors? It can be an exhilarating experience as you think about donors and how they have responded to your seminary. But while saying thank you is an enjoyable and essential step in expressing appreciation for gifts to your seminary, it also sets the stage for your next gift.

An appropriate thank you can act as an additional "ask," express your genuine appreciation for the gift, and demonstrate to others how they will be appreciated if they will give a similar gift.

Also, remember that when the gift is receipted in a timely manner and an appropriate thank you letter is sent, it will demonstrate that your organization is efficient, effective, and knowledgable. This will certainly encourage further giving.

As you design your plans for thanking donors, consider some of these guidelines.

1. Personalize. Personalize your acknowledgments as much as possible whether you are using letters, cards, postcards, acknowledgment receipts, or printed forms. If gifts are given to the computer fund, library, scholarships, or other designated funds, respond specifically and share with the donor how this advances the seminary's mission.

On pre-printed forms, you can personalize by writing in blue ink on the bottom something like "Thanks, John, for your important help."

Personalization also means being personal and telling stories. Tell the stories of your students, the churches they serve, and the good works that they do. Give the donors credit for allowing these good works to happen. These personal stories will add life and vitality to your letters of thanks.

2. Use others to write thank you letters. Your seminary has excellent resources in its secretaries, students, church members, graduates, key volunteers, and board members, who have benefited from the seminary's programs. International students can write exciting letters that will show your donors how their gifts provide benefits "beyond our shores."

3. Telephone your donors. A phone call is one of the most effective ways of saying "thank you" to the donor. Before the thank you letter is mailed, the donor may be called and thanked for the gift. The caller can confirm basic information such as address and intended purpose of the gift. This will give you the opportunity to learn something about the donor, such as approximate age, marital status, or information about the children. While you cannot always call all donors, you may select donors whose gifts meets certain qualifications each month, such as all new donors or gifts over a certain amount. Try to make some calls yourself with the balance shared by secretaries, other development staff, or the president.

4. Say thank you in person. Many development officers know how difficult it is to get out of their offices when they are overcome by paperwork and day-to-day management details. One of the easiest ways to get out and call on donors is to set aside an afternoon each week to hand deliver your acknowledgment receipts and letters. You will discover much useful information and you will be able to give donors the special attention they will appreciate.

5. Give donors a gift. Your seminary probably has an abundance of small gifts that can be provided to donors as a way of showing your appreciation. Faculty members have written books or booklets that donors would enjoy. You can reprint articles or send bookmarks, calendars, seminary tee shirts, cassette tapes from special services, or videotapes of seminary events.

6. Thank donors in print. List your donors in your publications and call special attention to innovative gifts. Always publish bequests received, if appropriate, as an encouragement and example for others to follow.

7. Honor significant donors. Hold a banquet, press conference, special chapel service, or other special event at which you honor significant donors. Form clubs for all levels of donations and welcome donors into these clubs by sending certificates, lapel pins, or other means of allowing the donor to feel a part of your organization.

8. Visit churches. When you visit churches in which donors are members, make special presentations to recognize them for their service to the church through the seminary.

9. Invite donors to tour with the president. Make donors feel a part of an exclusive group related to your seminary by inviting them to accompany the president on national or international tours.

10. Send donors invitations. Send donors invitations to special lectures, presentations, and other events. Send them tickets to special events and reserve seats and parking places for your special donors. Even if you are a national organization and do not anticipate them attending the event, it is still important to help the donor feel a part of your organization. For example, each invitation can include a paragraph that says "this event is made possible by the generous gifts of seminary donors."

Add your donors to a special "insider newsletter." This newsletter is especially for donors and gives them up-to-date information on your organization and shows them how their gifts are being used. Also, send them special financial planning newsletters and information on wills, bequests, trusts, and other planned gifts.

A fund raiser was asked how she raised so much money. She responded saying, "I get them to make the first gift and then I keep thanking them until they give again." Keep thanking your donors, for as the author William Feather has said, "Generous deeds would be repeated oftener if more gratitude had been shown for the first one."

Chapter Three:
Working With Foundations

Foundation Fund Raising:
Six Basic Principles

Daniel Schipp

There's no magic involved in persuading foundations that your seminary deserves support. It's mostly common sense and perseverance. Here are six practical principles to keep in mind as you seek foundation support for theological education.

1. Don't force a square peg into a round hole. Before you begin to put your proposal on paper, ask yourself a few questions: Is this project or program clearly consistent with my seminary's mission? Is it a priority for my institution? Does the program match the foundation's interest and philosophy of giving?

A negative response to any one of these questions tells you that you are trying to force a square peg into a round hole. Many excellent proposals are rejected because they don't match the foundation's current interests.

Check available sources to determine which foundations might be interested in your program. The first source to check is the foundation's annual report. Not all foundations are large enough to produce an annual report, but those that do will usually include in their report a statement about their philosophy of giving, guidelines for grant seekers, and a description of recently funded projects. Note that some larger foundations have a separate publication which outlines guidelines for submitting proposals.

Other sources of information about foundations and their interests are *The Foundation Directory, Source Book Profiles, Taft Foundation Report,* the *National Data Book of Foundations,* and the *Fund Raiser's Guide To Religious Philanthropy.*

Another way to determine if there is a match between your project and the foundation's priorities is to send a letter of inquiry to the foundation, describing in one or two pages your institution, the scope and objectives of the proposed project, and the probable budget.

Establishing up front that your "peg" fits the interests of the prospective foundation will save you time and frustration later on.

2. No hocus-pocus . . . just focus. In order to make the best use of your limited time and resources, concentrate on those foundations that are most likely to support your institution. Of the more than 22,000 active grant-making foundations, relatively few are serious prospects for your seminary.

Which are your best prospects? These categories of foundations come to mind:

A. Foundations of families with close ties to your institution. Have you identified the families among your constituents which have private foundations? If you have not, you may be missing out on a significant source of support. In our case, for example, of the eighteen foundations which made grants in the last two years, seven were family foundations.

B. Foundations within your community or state. The truism, "The closer you are to home, the better your chances for success," certainly applies to fund raising from foundations. Do not spend time tilting at the windmills of large national foundations unless they have expressed interest in theological education. Concentrate on those closest to your campus. During the last two years seventy-four percent of our total foundation support came from foundations in the state of Indiana.

C. National foundations with an interest in theological education. There are a few national foundations that have a record of support for religion and theological education. Notable among these foundations are Lilly Endowment, Booth Ferris, Arthur Vining Davis, Helms, Chatlos, Henry Luce, and Pew Charitable Trusts. Even with these foundations, make sure you understand their limits and priorities before you submit a proposal.

3. "Success" in proposal writing is spelled with five C's. After you have completed your research and identified the best prospective foundation(s) for your project, then (and only then!)

it is time to prepare the proposal. Keep in mind five C's as you write the proposal: make it credible, compelling, concise, consistent and complete.

Credible: In the proposal, especially in the introduction, you need to establish credibility. Build confidence in your institution's ability to carry out the proposed project by stating how long you have been in existence, the success you have had with similar projects, the breadth of your financial support, and your plans for the future and how this project relates to those plans.

Compelling: Build a compelling case for your project. Show how it will advance the mission of your seminary and the objectives of the foundation. State why the project is worthy of support. What benefits does it offer society? Why is it urgent?

Concise: It is important to involve the program expert(s)—dean, faculty member—in drafting the initial text. But you, as the development officer, must edit the text for readability, clarity, and conciseness. Avoid jargon and do not pad the proposal. Foundation officers appreciate economy of words.

Consistent: Test for consistency in your proposal. Ask an independent party to critique it. Ask this person to be especially watchful for contradiction and discrepancies in the information or budget.

Complete: It is essential that you provide the foundation with all the information that is required. Make sure that your proposal addresses each and every one of the foundation's guidelines.

4. Foundations are people. Foundations are not cold, impersonal organizations. As in other sources of philanthropy, people in foundations give grants to people they know and trust for the benefit of other people. Therefore, nurturing a relationship is as important in foundation raising as it is in raising funds from an individual. Honesty, openness, and respect are essential in that relationship. The more personal the relationship, the better; that is, a visit is better than a phone call, a phone call is better than a letter.

In cultivating a relationship with a foundation, pay particular attention to ongoing communication. Keep the foundation informed about your seminary's challenges, opportunities, and successes. Listen and respond to the foundation's concerns and interests. Provide the foundation with progress reports on the project it is supporting. Find appropriate ways to recognize the generosity of the foundation.

5. *"No" isn't forever.* If your proposal is turned down by the foundation, do not become disheartened. It is generally estimated that only seven percent of the nearly one million foundation proposals submitted each year are funded.

Most importantly, do not assume that you have been written off forever by the foundation. Go back a second time, a third time . . . a twelfth time, provided your program and the foundation's objectives match.

6. *Don't put all your eggs in the foundation basket.* One last word of advice. Keep in mind that in recent years six cents of the total philanthropic dollar came from foundations. You may want to budget your time and resources accordingly. Do not disregard foundations as a source of funding for theological education, but concentrate on the individuals —alums, parents, trustees and friends—who are responsible for nearly ninety percent of all philanthropy.

How to Work With Foundation Program Officers

Martin Paul Trimble

Very few private foundations maintain religious philanthropy programs and even fewer provide support for theological education. This situation makes program officers in religion an endangered species. It also insures that a strong communications network exists among the persons responsible for the religion grantmaking in the foundation community. We talk and meet regularly to discuss issues of mutual concern and to discern how our grantmaking might be appropriately coordinated. Such close interaction over the last three years with colleagues from the Lilly Endowment, Ford Foundation, and Trinity Church have been most rewarding and provide me with a perspective from which to comment generally on the most effective ways for prospective grantees to work effectively with this committed group of professionals. Several work rules apply:

Know the foundation's priorities. Before contacting the program officer at a foundation, be sure you have a clear understanding of the funder's goals and objectives. Guidelines and annual reports are published for a purpose: to provide prospective applicants with the parameters within which grants are made. A lot of time, energy, and good will can be conserved if the officer and grantee representatives do not have to review issues already fully explained in the foundation's public documents. Doing your homework up front allows the foundation and the seminary to continue to be good stewards of their resources of time and money.

Do not just send foundations a proposal. If, after reading the foundation's guidelines, you determine that a congruence of interests exists between the seminary and the funder, a seminary representative should make preliminary contact with the program officer to verify whether your impression is correct. It is best to start with a brief letter summarizing the project for which you need funding. Prospective grantees which do not have a prior history with the funder should include an annual report with this initial letter in order to give the program officer an overview of your organization's history and entire program. You should allow the program officer about a month to respond. If you do not receive a letter within this period, feel free to call. Blind calls not preceded by a letter are less helpful, for they usually catch the program officer off guard and do not provide him/her with adequate time to consider seriously the project in question.

Do not hesitate to ask for explicit instructions. When a foundation indicates an interest in reviewing a full proposal, the designated seminary representative should request specific instructions about the content and structure of the formal proposal. Most funders provide a checklist of information needed in order to process a grant application. Be sure to follow these instructions carefully. Attention to detail makes a good impression and avoids delays in considering your request.

Involve key persons. Involve the persons responsible for project design and management in the negotiations with the foundation. Because of their diverse responsibilities, development officers can only know a limited amount about the multitude of programs and projects for which they must raise money. Foundation officers welcome and usually insist on hearing from and working directly with those persons in the seminary responsible for the program idea, design, and management. Ideally, senior administrators at the seminary should endeavor to coordinate and facilitate this interaction, providing the technical support necessary for effective communication and partnership.

Speak your piece. Do not compromise your integrity. Seminary representatives should always deal forthrightly with funders and should insist on the same treatment in return. Do not craft your words or shape a project just to fit the guidelines of the foundation. Clearly, grantees need to be responsive to a foundation's program priorities and suggestions, but representatives should never compromise the integrity of the institution or the project just to receive a grant. If you believe a funder has seriously misjudged a project and can demonstrate specifically how your venture meets the needs of the constituency it is designed to serve, you should help the officer understand his or her miscalculation. Be prepared for healthy disagreement and differences of opinion. You may not persuade the officer about the correctness of your point of view, but he or she will respect you for having tried. Such respect will serve the seminary well with future funding requests.

Invite program officers to visit the project site. Fortunately, foundation representatives are intellectually curious and adventuresome persons. Usually, they are eager to visit project sites and the sponsoring institutions. Seminaries should extend invitations to officers to visit when they are certain the foundation's board will review a grant request. Hosts should treat a foundation guest without fanfare. The red carpet treatment and special orchestrated events are awkward and usually detract from the primary purpose of a site visit: talking and interacting with the persons responsible for and beneficiaries of the proposed project. Often, time constraints prevent a foundation officer from visiting every project. Do not be offended if your invitation is declined. Officers will most likely visit those projects where first-hand experience will help him or her to understand better the project in question.

Trust that the foundation officer is your advocate. Foundation officers are selected for their positions because of past experience in the field. Their judgment is highly valued by their employer and by the board to whom they are accountable. Prospective grantees should also know that the officer takes seriously his or her charge to serve the community. Program officers are prospective grantees' most vigorous advocates. It is wise to listen carefully to their advice and guidance. Viewing the proposal development process as a partnership which involves significant refinements of any grant application will save many frustrations. Trust that the officer has your best interest at heart when he or she makes suggestions about your proposal.

Rejoice with an approval. Be philosophical about a rejection. The demand for foundation funding is overwhelming. Most foundations approve less than ten percent of the grant requests they receive. If your institution receives encouragement to submit a full proposal, you should be cautiously optimistic that a grant might be made. Remember: foundation officers make recommendations and the board makes grants; therefore, there are no guarantees. In case of a rejection, you should expect and are entitled to a full explanation. After this has been provided, the seminary should monitor the foundation's guidelines closely for new opportunities for partnership. The rejection was for a project and not for the institution.

Adhere to program and financial reporting requirements exactly. After a grant is approved, the institution and the foundation have committed themselves to a significant relationship. A binding legal contract will rule and margin this partnership. Providing program and financial reports when requested is both a legal and ethical obligation. Failure to adhere exactly to the terms of the contract will erode the trust and good will between the foundation and grantee. Not taking reporting seriously will jeopardize the success of the funded project and future funding to the institution.

These suggestions are meant to serve as a general guide for seminary representatives who will work with foundations, including development personnel, presidents, trustees, faculty, and chief academic officers. They do not represent official policy of The Pew Charitable Trusts or any other foundation. Every foundation and its officers have their own ways of conducting business. Adjustments will be required in each situation. Overall, institutions should manage and track their foundation relations so that they develop an expertise and consistency which can be respected no matter what the context.

Foundation Giving
and Theological Education

Michaeline O'Dwyer, RSHM

What is the process followed prior to and after submitting a proposal to a foundation? The following is a process I recommend:

Know the goals and priorities of the institution. Talk with the president, dean, and faculty members in order to identify the areas where funding is needed to enhance or make possible a particular program. The development officer is not the one to decide where funding is needed. She or he is usually aware of certain foundations and their priorities and is often in a position to suggest some good funding sources. It is important to know the needs of the institution, support of faculty and/or others for the program or project, and the potential for funding. The program or project should be one that will have ongoing support from the institution after the grant period and is not one that becomes an expense project for the institution.

Know the resources to help identify appropriate foundations. The Foundation Center is a nonprofit organization established by foundations to provide reliable sources of information on private philanthropic giving. The Foundation Centers in Cleveland, New York City, San Francisco, and Washington, DC, offer many services such as workshops on researching foundations and effective use of the Center as well as a comprehensive collection of information on foundations and grants. In other cities, libraries, community foundations, state universities, and nonprofit agencies provide a core collection of Foundation Center publications, supplementary materials, and services useful to grant seekers. Collections include a wide variety of directories, guides, annual reports, and the IRS 990-PF returns of private foundations.

Foundation directories are practical tools to use in identifying appropriate foundations. Some directories are general in nature while others are subject-oriented: grants for women, for individuals, for religious organizations. The indexes are very helpful because they list foundations under headings such as recipient type, recipient state, geographic or religious preference; officers and directors are listed alphabetically and include the foundation(s) on which they serve.

Some examples of directories are the *Foundation Reporter, Fund Raiser's Guide to Religious Philanthropy,* and *Corporate Giving Directory* published by The Taft Group; and *The Foundation Directory, Foundation Grants to Individuals,* and *The Foundation Grants Index* published by The Foundation Center.

Directories are expensive. Before purchasing any, it is wise to consider which ones will be the most useful for the development office. Space the purchase of directories over a period of two or three budget years, replace as needed, and use the Foundation Center collections to supplement or to cross-check your office collection.

Other publications. Annual reports, published by many foundations, are available for the asking. Many give information on number and size of grants, grantees, and projects funded. *The Chronicle of Philanthropy, The Chronicle of Higher Education,* and the *Foundation Giving Watch* are sources of recent grants and other information related to fund raising.

Past files. A review of the past history of the institution's relationship with a foundation often proves helpful when trying to make new connections.

Conferences and workshops are also helpful, particularly those on foundation and corporate giving and on writing proposals.

Other people from similar or different institutions, and from conferences or workshops are excellent sources of information.

Research. Identify those foundations that will give to

seminaries, theological education, religious education, higher education, or to a particular program or project. Look for similar situations where funding has been granted in the past.

Devise a foundation profile form, use it to record significant information on foundations; keep a hard copy and computer file. In doing the research, first look at the foundation's priorities, limitations, and restrictions to see if there is a fit and then review the asset base, number and average size of grants, grantees, and projects; trustees and directors; application procedures; deadlines. Send for any foundation publications listed: annual report, public policy statement, application guidelines. Periodically send a list of foundation officers and directors to the institution's trustees asking them to review the list, mark those whom they know or may have some connection with, and return the marked list to the development office.

Use and update research as needed. Get to know certain foundations.

Approach a foundation. When the research has been completed, begin the process of building a relationship with the foundation. Work together on a common interest, not on a laundry list of requests. How to do this depends on the policy of the foundation. Determine whether or not the foundation grants visits. If it doesn't, follow the guidelines with regard to sending a proposal or request. If the guidelines make no reference to visits, phone and ask for an appointment with the foundation's contact person (not with an officer or director!) to talk about the institution, its mission, program, or project, as well as to learn more about the work of the foundation itself. In some cases, it may be only a phone visit. In others an appointment will be made. The visit itself will vary with the style of the person visited, i.e., the length of the visit, what is talked about, direction or advice given. Listen carefully to what is said. It could be significant in preparing the proposal.

Immediately after the meeting, write a letter thanking the person for the opportunity to visit. If appropriate, add the foundation to the development office mailing list to receive the institution's newsletter or other similar publications.

Write the proposal; put it together with all materials requested by the foundation in a simple and presentable form.

After the proposal has been sent, continue contact with the foundation by sending related information on the grant project or about the institution, i.e., other grants received, news articles, talks.

Make connections. Use the connections between institution trustees and foundation directors as appropriate. Phone the trustee, send a copy of the proposal and ask him or her to write to the foundation contact in support of the institution and its request. Keep the institution trustee informed on any progress on the grant proposal.

Practice good stewardship. The foundation will either award or not award a grant. If not, write a brief letter acknowledging review of the proposal. In some cases, it may be beneficial to call the contact person at the foundation and ask if there were specific reasons for denial of the proposal. When, happily, a grant is awarded, write a letter of thanks, reemphasize the importance of the project and the funding, and include response to any conditions or agreements made by the foundation.

During the grant period continue to send information on the project or the institution to the foundation.

Interim and final reports to the foundation must be on time, thoughtful, and complete. Include evaluations and/or reports written by those who profited from the program funded; send photos, video, or other materials when suitable.

Have those who benefited directly from a grant, e.g., students who received scholarships, write letters of thanks addressed to the appropriate person at the foundation.

Publicize the program, the funding, and the foundation in a suitable manner, unless the foundation asks for confidentiality.

In summary, acknowledge the foundation personally and specially, as with all other benefactors!

The "Forgotten" Foundation and One Way to Reach It

Richard Eppinga

Many planned giving workshops denigrate charitable gift annuities as more trouble than they are worth, as suitable only for the small-potato "mom-and-pop" operations, and generally as a distraction from really important things like trusts.

In fact charitable gift annuities often are the best solution as well as the easiest. Some of the "mom-and-pop" operations turn out not to be so small after all. Charitable gift annuities indeed have been worth the attention of Calvin Seminary.

Now here is a parallel situation. Many foundation workshops concentrate on large foundations with extensive professional staffs and well-defined, published policies and procedures. Non-profit organizations spend big time going after big foundations for big grants.

But there is another foundation that too often is overlooked. I would like to encourage us to be contrarians and to consider a "forgotten" foundation (the small, private foundation) as worth our interest and attention.

The glamour of the national foundation and its large, sought-after grants can obscure the significance of the "small" private foundation, the permanent charitable trust, and the testamentary trust. Yet sometimes the latter are more accessible to and more sympathetic toward the theological school than the former. Strategies to reach them can pay satisfying dividends to those who invest in their cultivation. This article investigates one practical approach.

We all know of the Ford Foundation, the Kellogg Foundation, and the Kresge, Rockefeller, and Mellon Foundations. Through ATS and DIAP we know about the largesse of the Lilly Endowment and its special interest in religion. And we are fortunate to have The Pew Charitable Trusts supporting theological education. These foundations count their assets in billions of dollars.

There are hundreds of foundations with assets in the hundreds of millions. There are more than two thousand foundations with assets of $10 million or more. (Paul Ylvisaker, in his seminal 1989 Occasional Paper entitled "Small Can Be Effective" for the Council on Foundations, uses $10 million as the dividing line between large and small foundations.)

But there are almost 25,000 foundations with assets of less than $10 million dollars—most of them much, much less. Every one of them gives away money. Even a family foundation with a few thousand dollars of assets gives away money.

For the purposes of Calvin Seminary, with only a very few exceptions, a small foundation is any foundation with whom we work. If we work with it or at it, it is small by definition.

We have compiled a list of the foundations that have a special tie to our institution. Our special tie is this—virtually all the principals of these foundations are or once were members of the denomination that established and maintains our seminary—the Christian Reformed Church. There are around fifty foundations on our list. Only two have assets of more than $10 million. When we know the assets at all, and for most we do not, the range is from a few thousand dollars to a few hundred thousand. Our list of fifty constitutes, essentially, our grant universe. In recent years the Lilly Endowment and The Pew Charitable Trusts are the only large, well-known national foundations that have given us a grant.

What can the foundations do for us? This is a simple question to answer. These foundations can help us by giving us their money. They know that. We know that. But every coin has two sides. The other side of this coin is the more difficult question. But we believe it holds an answer to the first question.

The second question is what can we do for the foundations? What can Calvin Seminary do for these foundations that will elicit the support from them that we need?

We do as many of the usual things as we can. Recently we did one not-so-usual thing. Calvin Seminary offered a foundation seminar.

Why did we do it? Small foundations can use the assistance. Helping them helps us. Helping them builds God's kingdom. Small foundations are grateful for aid. Many foundations do not have professional staffs and are governed by the people who established them and donate to them, with perhaps an additional family member or two and the periodic assistance of an attorney and accountant.

We wanted to offer a foundation seminar or workshop to those who had small private family or business foundations. That required money. Our foundation seminar cost $5,000 that we did not have in our annual budget.

Providentially we got the money—from the Lilly Endowment. The foundation seminar was included in one of two grant proposals we submitted to Lilly, both of which were funded. The one grant, for $75,000, was for faculty scholarship and service. This $75,000 included $25,000 for financial development with the goal of establishing an endowment to fund faculty scholarship and service. Of the $25,000 we requested and received for financial development, we proposed, received, and expended $5,000 on the foundation seminar.

Naturally we wanted as much benefit as possible from the seminar. Who else would benefit from a foundation seminar? The answer was persons who have established charitable trusts. Therefore we entitled the seminar "Foundations, Trusts, and Christian Stewards."

Why add charitable trusts? There are several reasons. First, there are lots of them. We knew of seminary friends who had trusts and we suspected others of having them. There are different types of charitable trusts, including some that presently do not even exist—a testamentary trust comes into existence at death. Second, charitable trusts provide about two-thirds of the planned gifts given to charitable institutions (see "Charitable Remainder Trusts," National Committee on Planned Giving,

1994). Third, just like foundation principals, trustees can use advice. Trustees, too, have charitable fiduciary responsibilities. They file forms. Like foundation principals, they require legal and financial assistance. Fourth, interestingly, a permanent charitable trust legally can be called a foundation.

In proposing the seminar, we envisioned that its ambiance would be personalized and attuned to the interests and needs of its participants. The emphasis would be on quality rather than quantity and involve only fifteen to twenty-five persons. The seminar would be "first-class" in every respect—resource persons, presentations, meeting rooms, accommodations, and meals—with as many "extra touches" as possible. It would be friendly, informal, and unthreatening in tone. Finally it would be clear to all that the seminar was offered to participants as a service with the goal of the advancement of God's kingdom. There would be no financial solicitation and there would be no obligation to the seminary.

We chose a date with a minimum of conflicts in late October—a pleasant time in western Michigan. The seminar was scheduled on a Thursday and Friday, facilitating transportation and allowing the incorporation of a weekend if the participants so desired. For facilities we chose a fine hotel and convention center near the seminary and near the airport that is owned in part by a seminary friend.

The accommodations were luxury rooms, not standard rooms. Rather than eating in a conference room, we made certain that participants ordered from the menu and dined in the excellent restaurant—something unexpected and greatly appreciated by our guests. At all times in our meeting room during the two-day seminar we ensured an abundance of beverages and food—including desserts.

More than three months in advance of the seminar the seminary president personally called the persons on the lists we had prepared. We followed up with written materials. Soon we thought we had the number of people we wanted. As noted later, this was a mistake. In the two weeks prior to the seminar we did much telephoning and faxing to fill the seminar.

The seminar itself went well. Attendance was within the range for which we had planned. Accommodations, meeting rooms, food, and drink were first-class. With one exception the presentations were excellent and well-received.

We had a budget and, as with all budgets, we were high in some areas and low in others. But the bottom line was close to where it should have been—only $150 over our $5,000 budget.

There was one large and unfortunate problem—video-taping—that turned our careful planning and budgeting upside down.

Do we consider the seminar a success? Yes. Would we do it again? Yes. Calvin Seminary was of unique service to important and sometimes overlooked friends and constituents.

All who were present enjoyed themselves, plain and simple. Good surroundings, good information, good fellowship, good food. Every person involved, participants and presenters alike, thanked us for a uniquely enjoyable experience.

Participants and presenters alike told us that they felt edified, uplifted, and encouraged by the seminar.

Participants received vital information for which they were grateful. Here is but one example. Many did not know that they faced the imminent demise of a crucially important tax break for gifts of appreciated stock to private foundations. Legislation allowing the deductibility of such gifts at market value expired December 31, 1994. As of January 1, 1995, donors can deduct only their cost basis.

At the time and since the seminar, we received many requests for seminar videotapes.

Would we do anything differently if we had the opportunity? Yes.

We would start even earlier with the invitations and maintain regular contact with would-be attendees, in order to ensure their attendance. Despite our best efforts to the contrary, some invitees likely were skeptical of our motivation or did not want to feel obligated to contribute to us at some later date. Too many who had agreed to attend canceled as the date approached, some with scant notice, forcing us to scramble to fill the gaps. There were more cancellations from persons at a distance than among those closer by, suggesting that the cost of air transportation may have tipped the balance.

We would stick to our original plan to do the videotaping ourselves, utilizing seminary equipment, supplies, and student editing. A last-minute decision to engage a commercial service was an expensive mistake.

When the seminar originally was envisioned, we could answer the question "Will it pay for itself?" only with an opinion—"We think so in the long run; we hope so in the short run." Today we have evidence that the seminar did pay for itself as a result of actions taken by several participants and presenters:

Some in attendance gave new or larger-than-usual gifts to the seminary.

Some presenters refused their honorarium or donated it at the end of the year.

A person has established a family scholarship for the seminary.

A person informed us that the seminary will receive a foundation gift this year from her foundation.

A person stated to us that he is naming the seminary as a beneficiary in his charitable remainder unitrust.

A person established an endowed seminary lecture series.

We expect to discover this year and into the future additional happy results of the seminar.

We are grateful to the Lilly Endowment for making possible our seminar for "Foundations, Trusts, and Christian Stewards." The experience has reinforced our belief that, as important as are the large national foundations, Calvin Seminary should expend the greater portion of its foundation efforts upon the "forgotten" foundations—the small private foundations with which it enjoys unique accessibility and sympathy.

The Hidden Costs of Grants

Bruce C. Stewart

A free toothbrush! That's what the coupon said. So I went to the nearest drugstore, presented the coupon and walked out with a new toothbrush.

When I got home I found that the handle was thicker than the slot in the toothbrush holder. That meant getting a new toothbrush holder But the new toothbrush holder didn't match the soap dish, and the style of the new toothbrush holder and soap dish rather demanded a new decor in the sink and cabinets.

Many times we have received generous grants from foundations only to find that additional costs generated by the new equipment or facilities or programs impacted negatively upon other parts of our budget. How can we communicate to foundations this pressure that we experience so that there can be mutual sensitivity to this concern?

There are times when we as seminaries may fear that adding incremental or subsequent costs to a proposal may make the proposal less attractive or competitive; therefore we may omit things like maintenance, utilities, office expense, and other overhead costs even though this may place great strains upon items already in our budgets.

Lance Buhl, writing in *Foundation News* (Jan.-Feb. 1986), says that this fear "is greatly increased by the failure of many foundations . . . to publish their indirect cost rules or budget making guidelines." It would indeed be helpful to know if and which indirect costs are allowed or encouraged by the foundation.

As a small seminary we welcome grants of any size, but it would often be true that some grants produce a small net income. Hidden costs such as personnel time in research, conferences, writing and revising proposals and cover letters, and submitting follow-up reports can consume a large percentage of the grant. How many of these hidden costs should we include in a proposal?

Some years ago the Hunt family in Pittsburgh offered an extensive collection of botanical books to the Carnegie Library. This offer was refused by the library because they did not have room to house the collection. Then the offer was made to Carnegie-Mellon University (then Carnegie Tech); the administration said they would accept the collection if the Hunt family would construct and endow a building to house it. To this the Hunt family agreed. There are more recent examples of this kind of negotiation and response.

Some government grants to universities provide eighty percent, ninety percent, and even one hundred percent for indirect costs. Perhaps we as seminaries need to explore and encourage such possibilities.

In some cases, hidden costs may accrue because proposals fail correctly to anticipate subsequent costs. For example, we presented a proposal last spring to a foundation for a significant increase in personal computers, software, terminals, and printers for our library. We had preliminary conversations with the director of the foundation and presented our proposal within the guidelines of the foundation. We were both pleased and thankful when the foundation granted everything we asked for. However, after everything was in place we found that the increased usage made our computer memory inadequate, and that we needed to double the megabytes in the main frame. This was for us a hidden cost that we should have anticipated and included in the proposal.

This raises another issue. It is probably unrealistic for us to expect more funding to meet something overlooked in our proposal, but is the policy of many foundations justified in refusing support in subsequent years? Few successful programs are built all at once. Essential development and maintenance also require new dollars. If the foundation likes what we're doing they can help us succeed by several years of support. Even when all costs have correctly been anticipated there are additional costs which may need to be funded. Would there be wisdom in including multi-year funding in our proposals?

Still another suspect guilty of hidden costs is the challenge grant or gift match. While this may have a tremendous appeal to many donors, it also draws funds from those who might have given more to pressing needs of the school.

A seminary president told me this week of a challenge grant for a new dormitory. A handsome gift came in from a donor who expressed great interest in the project but indicated also that he would not be able to contribute to the annual fund this year. Since he was one of the largest donors to the annual fund, this assumed critical proportions.

Unfortunately, most foundations do not offer grants to things as mundane as operating expense, not even challenge grants. It's a rare foundation that gives to a school's highest priorities. Their objectives are usually quite significant, but their value lessens if the grant leaves the seminary in a weaker position financially than before the grant was made.

There are times when the hidden costs of grants can be justified. The grant may be our first relationship with the foundation and may be seen as a step toward more substantial support. Or the grant from a particular foundation may give prestige to the seminary and open the door to other foundations.

Certainly, we need to recognize that many developments have been initiated by start-up costs provided by foundations or by grants that set in motion things that we really needed. Without that foundation support we may have lacked the incentive as well as the funds to put valuable programs into place.

So we need to express our deep appreciation for foundation grants. We have willingly received them despite hidden costs. We have been stretched for our own good. Yet I would conclude with two recommendations: that we be astute enough not to be swayed in our objectives by the whims of foundations, and that we be bold enough to ask foundations to consider underwriting more of the indirect/hidden costs of grants.

Chapter Four:
Planned Giving

Planned Giving is Not an Option

Bill L. Barnes

Planned giving is an established ingredient in the funding arsenal of only thirty-four percent of the accredited seminaries in the United States and Canada. Yet those schools with such programs, small or large, receive forty-five percent of their income from gifts and grants compared to thirty-two percent for schools without planned giving programs. Institutions with planned giving programs garner an average of more than four hundred percent the gift income received by institutions without such programs.

In a time when attention is being given to the financial profile and performance of seminaries, it behooves all seminaries to consider how they can realize greater productivity from their development efforts. Recent studies indicate that there is no more potentially productive arena for additional attention than planned giving.

Operating costs of such programs are, of course, a crucial factor in launching such efforts. There is a dramatic difference in the registered achievements of schools with full-time leadership in planned giving as compared to those institutions with only part-time staff assigned to this function. However, even a carefully designated portion of a staff person's time for planned giving can demonstrably affect the total financial performance realized. The facts also indicate that planned giving makes a positive impact on other related development achievements as well.

Those institutions in 1984-85 that marshaled significant infusions of new dollars for their programs invested about twenty-one percent of all their fund raising and development dollars in the planned giving enterprise. The more productive of these institutions designated about $60,000 a year to this effort. Other schools in earlier stages of designing and implementing their planned giving programs directed as modest an amount as ten percent of their funding budgets to that program facet. However, the cautious approach has been lethal to the program when it is continuously restricted in its ability to move toward full-time leadership and sufficient program resources.

Smaller schools have the same obligations to their constituencies regarding investment opportunities as larger institutions. Planned giving programs provide such counsel and thereby open up opportunities with the potential to explode microscopic financial gestures into massive financial blessings.

How soon do such efforts provide income to a school? This depends upon how intensively and completely the institution is committed to the process. It normally is concretely reflected within five years. Over a ten-year period, a planned giving program proves to be one of the wisest investments made by a seminary. It is as important an investment as the management of institutional endowments!

There will be those schools, however, that will need to start such programming with more limited resources. But even then there will be some immediate benefit in terms of the seminary's ability to relate responsibly to its constituency, to sharpen the focus of the school's leadership relative to its financial responsibilities, and adequately to reflect its mission and the way in which it is being addressed.

The function of the seminary is fundamental to the proclamation of the gospel. Seminaries dare not hold back those processes that create greater capacity for persons to give and to express the love that they have toward other people and the church as they take seriously the message of the gospel.

Planned giving is not an option! It is an essential for every seminary. Those schools that have invested in this kind of endeavor find that they are securing resources at a cost of nine to twelve cents per dollar. Responsible stewardship demands that seminaries take seriously this essential ingredient in modern educational and church funding.

How to Start
a Deferred Giving Program

Donovan J. Palmquist

Every institution has a deferred giving program, although many do not recognize it. Deferred giving, in its basic form, is the decision by a donor to give a gift which will be received at a later time by the institution. Often, we are so busy seeking gifts for "now" that we give little attention to the "later" gifts.

There are four ways to give a gift:

1. cash or other gifts of value,
2. a gift which provides a life income for the donor,
3. a gift by which the institution uses a person's money for a time, receives the interest, and returns the principal to the lender, and
4. a gift through a will.

The goal of a deferred giving program is to focus the last three of these methods in a systematic way.

The key steps in organizing a deferred giving program include:

Learn. Become knowledgeable about deferred giving. Counsel with someone who has a successful program, attend a deferred giving conference, read the literature, and become acquainted with your denomination's foundation or program.

Identify. Identify those persons whom you know have included your institution in their estate plans. Call on them to thank them and keep them informed about the seminary. Nurture their interest, for they are your best prospects for other gifts.

Plan. Develop a year-round plan to identify others who may be interested. Use the institution's publications to explain what deferred giving is. Include a clip-out coupon for more information. In annual fund mailings, particularly reply envelopes, include a place to indicate interest in deferred giving. Plan mailings to donors which provide information about ways to give. Keep the reader in mind and translate technical language (e.g. annuity, trust, unitrusts, etc.) into words everyone can understand. Speak of Christian stewardship, caring for one's resources, sharing with loved ones and in causes in which they believe.

List. Develop a list of the top fifty to one hundred prospects, based on their interest, commitment and resources. Gather basic information about these prospects: their relationship to your school, their resources, their interests. Note people who may be key "links" for you with these persons. Every three to six months review your prospect list with key people from the development staff and with the president.

Visit. Call on the prospects beginning with the top ten. Continue to gather information about the persons. Give them suggestions of ways to give which will fulfill their goals. Show them how to give to institutions without taking away from family. Be available to meet with their financial counselor, attorney, or others who give them advice. Invite them to campus. Have the president call on them. Remember special days in their lives. Become their friends. Be ready to make return visits.

Celebrate. Celebrate their gift. Secure their permission to announce it and publish their story. Ask others to thank them. Some institutions have a Heritage Society for those who have made commitments and give a special gift which is symbolic of the commitment.

Get help. Identify resources available to you. Not every seminary can have a full-time staff member for deferred giving. Contact denominational foundations and seminary friends who are "agents of wealth" for those who may be prospects.

Make it work. Refine and rework your plans for organizing your deferred giving program. The best program is the one that works for *you.*

Wait. Finally, do not grow weary in well doing. Some experts say it takes three to five years to realize results. Whatever the length of time, it is well spent because it represents a lifetime of investments, values, and visions.

Elements of a Planned Giving Program

Chase S. Hunt

The following are thoughts, borne of experience, regarding the establishing and sustaining of a planned giving program that will serve our institutions well. They presuppose a solid commitment on the part of the institution to have such a program as a part of its overall development activity, and the presence on staff of one who would carry out the planned giving responsibility.

The highly relational nature of planned giving calls for particular personal qualities on the part of the planned giving officer. Among these are:

a genuine interest in people that comes through as sincere and authentic;

a sensitivity to the needs and concerns of others;

enthusiasm about your institution and your role in representing it;

a strong sense of loyalty to your institution and the cause you represent;

a sense of humor to help you through unhappy or disappointing times, and the ability to learn and bounce back from them.

Note that the above listing does not include technical knowledge or skills that relate to this discipline. They are certainly desirable, but are of relatively little value apart from the personal qualities mentioned. Skills can be learned and information mastered. The personal traits are ingrained and are, in my view, of primary importance.

Now on to elements of a more general nature that contribute to a comprehensive, balanced planned giving program.

Essential Items in Establishing a Sound Program

Support of the board of trustees and the backing of your president. Without trustee and president support, the enterprise is seriously flawed from the start. It is imperative that the trustees and president recognize that the establishing of a planned giving program is an investment of effort and resources that will require time to develop and be of lasting benefit to the institution. There is a fundamental difference in the rhythm of an annual giving program and a planned giving program. The former is governed by the calendar, and its activity follows a predictable schedule with year-end deadlines. The latter is dependent upon the situations of individual donors whose gifts come when the time seems right to them given their various considerations, not according to a calendar or an institutional schedule.

Cooperation of your financial officer. It is important that both the planned giving officer and financial officer appreciate the concerns and needs of the other and work cooperatively with one another. Care should be taken to establish procedures that address business office and development considerations, and that serve the donor in timely fashion as well.

Access to competent legal/financial advice. This is vital to planned giving. Because of the tax and legal ramifications of gifts of this type, such advice when called for is in the best interest of both the institution and the donor. Donors should also be encouraged to consult with their own legal/financial advisors when contemplating entering into a planned giving arrangement.

Adequate budget to undergird your efforts. Results of planned gifts are not realized overnight. Often it is years before a particular gift actually becomes available to the institution. It is important that the program be funded, and equally important that it not be undermined by impatience and/or bottom-line considerations.

Opportunities for training to get started in planned giving, with continuing education along the way. Those entering planned giving as a profession come from a wide variety of backgrounds—some with legal or accounting experience and others from the pastorate or from faculty or administrative positions. To the extent that training in planned giving is needed, it should be made available through courses on the subject, seminars, or from individual instructors as may seem appropriate. Provision for such training and for continuing education should be made in the institution's annual budget as a matter of routine. It is money well spent.

Institutional Resources to
Equip and Support the Planned Giving Officer

A planned giving officer should be well acquainted with the mission of his or her organization as expressed in a carefully conceived and drawn mission statement. It is desirable that the preparation of such a statement have the benefit of input from the trustees, faculty, administrators, and student body in its formulation.

A planned giving policy statement adopted by the board of trustees. One indication of trustee support referred to earlier is the formal adoption of a policy statement that expresses the institution's commitment to the planned giving activity. A typical document would consist of three parts: the formal policy stating the objectives, guidelines, administrative and other considerations; a statement of procedural and management considerations; and a listing and description of the arrangements to be included in the institution's planned giving portfolio.

A thorough knowledge of the distinctive features of the institution. The planned giving officer should know the history of the organization, those who serve on the faculty and administration and the unique contribution they make to the institution, and the distinctive characteristics of the student body. Such information should be a source of pride to those of us who represent our institutions and interpret them to our constituents.

A ready awareness of the immediate and long-range goals and needs of the institution. A planned giving representative should never be caught off guard by the friend or donor who asks, "Just what is it that the seminary needs, and how can I help?"

A Working Knowledge
of the Technical Aspects of Planned Giving

Relevant tax laws and provisions. While the relational abilities of a planned giving officer are of key importance, it is important to become conversant with the technical side as well. Where taxes are concerned, an understanding of income tax, capital gains tax, gift and estate taxes, and the generation skipping tax, among others, is necessary. So, too, are tax provisions of your state and changes in federal and state tax laws as they occur.

An understanding of the instruments included in the institution's planned giving portfolio. Wills and bequests are the foundation of any planned giving program. That is a given. There are, in addition, other instruments and life income plans that make up the portfolio of a charitable institution. A typical planned giving portfolio would include the following:

      charitable gift annuity

      deferred payment gift annuity

      pooled income fund

      charitable remainder trusts

      charitable lead trusts

      retained life estate

      life insurance

Those engaged in planned giving for institutions such as ours should be well-acquainted with these arrangements and their distinctive characteristics. It is also important to be aware of and in conformity with any special requirements of your state with regard to offering these arrangements.

IRS discount rate and its influence on the charitable deduction; the relationship between payout of a particular planned giving vehicle and the charitable deduction. A planned giving officer should understand and be able to explain to a donor the effect on the charitable deduction of a higher or lower discount rate, and of a larger or smaller payout.

Principles of estate planning. Those of us who serve theological institutions may not be estate planners with certification and the like, but an understanding of the principles of that discipline will make us more effective in service to our institutions and our donors.

Marketing a Planned Giving Program

"A city built on a hill cannot be hid. No one after lighting a lamp puts it under the bushel basket. . . ." So states our Lord in the Sermon on the Mount. Neither should we develop a planned giving program at our institution and put it "under a bushel basket," but "on a lamp stand" for all to see. Marketing is one of the key elements of a well-rounded planned giving program. It can be accomplished in a number of ways.

Systematic mailings to donors/prospects. Such mailings are sent quarterly or at other intervals to those who have been identified as being likely individuals to receive information of this type. The content of such mailings varies from institution to institution, providing ample opportunity for creativity and innovation.

Brochures/booklets/ newsletters. These come in all sizes and shapes, and in varying degrees of sophistication. Some institutions write and publish their own material. Others purchase them from firms that produce such materials and have their logos imprinted on them, while still others choose the middle road of having copy for brochures or newsletters written for them which they further customize. Whatever your preference, there is wisdom in avoiding texts that are too technical and discouraging to the reader.

Articles in institutional publications. Quarterly alum publications and/or periodicals directed to other constituencies provide opportunity to include an article or feature story that highlights your institution's planned giving program. This works well for the institution I serve, where each issue of our two quarterly magazines features a brief article on a topic related to planned giving.

Articles in local newspapers. Some institutions are successful in having articles or stories published in local newspapers or other publications that feature a gift received or a personality or program associated with the institution. I take the view that any article which lifts up your institution and presents it in a positive light is beneficial. You never know how a particular item about the institution will strike people and prompt them to give it their support. The systematic preparation of press releases sent to local and regional newspapers would seem, then, to be time well spent.

Advertisements. Advertisements that feature the planned giving opportunities available through your institution give you the opportunity to direct such information to a particular audience in publications of your choosing. When done with care and imagination, they can be quite effective. From cartoons to more traditional ads to classifieds, this means of presenting your institution to its various publics and highlighting planned giving possibilities in the process is worthy of consideration in marketing your program.

Support Groups and
Opportunities for Personal Growth

There are times when the planned giving activity can seem a lonely one. The requirement of travel, sometimes for extended periods, separates us from our support base—our family and development colleagues at our institution. The following are organizations and activities that I have found helpful in broadening that support base through the forming of valued and lasting friendships, and important in providing opportunity for professional growth.

Our annual DIAP seminars. These occasions have given me the opportunity to become acquainted with colleagues serving other theological institutions and to experience the sharing of information and sharpening of skills that characterize these events.

American Council on Gift Annuities (ACGA). I especially appreciate the ACGA meetings held every three years, and the information and services this organization makes available in the interim.

Council for the Advancement and Support of Education (CASE). Several CASE conferences are held each year on a variety of topics that relate to development for educational institutions. I found them especially helpful in the early years of my planned giving activity and before the National Committee on Planned Giving came into existence.

National Committee on Planned Giving (NCPG). A relative newcomer, this organization is growing dramatically. Membership in local chapters offers the opportunity to join the national organization as well, which I find very beneficial. At meetings of the local chapters, friendships are formed and information is shared through presentations on timely subjects. The annual seminar offered by the NCPG is outstanding.

National Society of Fund Raising Executives (NSFRE). This organization is similar to the NCPG in its format of a national organization with local chapters. A distinctive feature is its certification program that results in the CFRE designation for those who meet the requirements. That program is well worth exploring.

Mentor and/or development colleagues. While I never had a mentor relationship, I wish I had, especially during my early years in planned giving, and recommend it to those who are new in the field. I have had the benefit of friendship and sharing with colleagues in development, however, both at my own institution and elsewhere, and am grateful for all that they have meant to me over the years. I have been especially impressed by the ready willingness of these colleagues to share ideas and materials and planned giving strategies, and to find joy in each others' successes. In response, I, like you, try to pass it along.

One further comment. In recent years, those engaged in the planned giving enterprise have felt a strong desire to protect the profession from unethical practices, real or perceived. As a result a statement, entitled *Model Standards of Practice for the Charitable Gift Planner,* was drawn up and formally adopted by both the American Council on Gift Annuities and the National Committee on Planned Giving. Both individuals and institutions may subscribe to these standards and I commend them to one and all.

The Anatomy of a Planned Gift:
The Five C's

Kim Clark

Many seminaries have yet to venture into the field of planned giving. Those who have will tell you that it is never too late and never too soon to begin a sustained marketing campaign for major planned gifts. Planned giving is generally defined as the act of making outright or deferred gifts in light of one's overall estate and financial plans. Often these gifts require the assistance of professional advisors. As more and more of the American population begin to age, planned giving will become central to continuing financial support of our institutions. Furthermore, various published studies have shown that in times of economic downturn, more of an institution's support comes from deferred gifts, including life income arrangements and bequests.

Major planned gift fund development today requires careful management and nurturing of relationships with existing and potential major contributors comprised primarily of older donors. One key factor in planned giving is to understand and maintain contact with better donors as they age. After they reach a certain age, typically sixty-five to seventy, it is important to monitor these relationships more carefully. One must be prepared to help older persons make what current gifts they can still make, while they are also in the process of contemplating what may be their largest gift of a lifetime through their estates. A recent outright planned gift to Pacific School of Religion epitomizes the anatomy of a planned gift. This gift illustrates what I have come to recognize as the Five C's in the major planned gift fund development process.

The Technique

Comfort. Long, sustained contact with the prospective donor is important, even after a gift is made. Continue the exposure to your institution in meaningful ways that raise the donor's comfort level with your institution and its mission. This differs from "cultivation" in that continuous personal contact is emphasized: hand addressed invitations and cards; frequent telephone calls; personal, informative notes identifying items of interest occurring at your institution; taking the donor out to dinner; et cetera.

Convenience. Keep the institutional advancement team visible within the active community from which your supporters are drawn. Have the president, the fund raising officers, and the faculty attend annual denominational conferences, preferably in leadership roles (e.g., lecturer, presenter, keynote speaker, host of an event, et cetera). Make it convenient for your supporters to mention any gift plans they are contemplating.

Coordination. Once a gift intention has been mentioned to an advancement team member, that member becomes the lead person to gather relevant information about the prospective donor. Coordinate this effort with others on the team by including a key volunteer or trustee who knows the prospect's capability to give. Or, this effort could be the responsibility of other team members who have been maintaining contact with the prospect and know the prospect's interests or who can provide technical expertise on gift plans.

Communication. Meet with the prospective donor to listen for the donor's concerns and areas of interest as well as to speak of gift opportunities that will meet the donor's expressed needs. Remember, this should be a discussion of mutual benefits.

Commitment. The gift results from the donor's understanding of your institution, its programs, and how his or her financial contribution can further that cause.

The Application

Comfort. Marian Western (not her real name) first came

to Pacific School of Religion in 1979 when she and her husband gave a modest outright gift to the seminary's campaign. Because of their ages, seventy and seventy-three, they became prime planned giving prospects. The planned giving officer at that time began a series of personal and sustained contacts with the donors which included letters, visits, planned giving newsletters, and invitations to events held at the seminary. Five years later, the Westerns' comfort level had moved to the place where they made a $10,000 gift to the PSR pooled income fund.

Convenience. Many years passed with the Westerns giving only occasional modest gifts to the seminary. No one thought at the time that an additional substantial gift would result. Yet in October 1994, Mrs. Western attended the annual fall Lay Leadership Conference where the vice president for institutional advancement was presenting a session. At the close of the day, Mrs. Western mentioned to the vice president that she had received an inheritance and wondered how she could use it to benefit PSR.

Coordination. Immediately, the planned giving officer met with the vice president to determine the donor's possible gift options, given her areas of interest and previous giving levels. Possible life income plans were discussed, including additional pooled income fund contributions.

Communication. A meeting with Mrs. Western was scheduled and a letter describing possible gift options was mailed in advance for her consideration. At the meeting Mrs. Western expressed interest in the matching fund challenge grant PSR had received to endow field education stipends.

Commitment. A few days later, a letter came in the mail from Mrs. Western. Enclosed was a check for $50,000 to be matched dollar for dollar, making her gift worth $100,000 to PSR! In light of her overall financial and estate planning needs, Mrs. Western had concluded that a gift of the inheritance she had received would benefit PSR in a way that could be doubled with the challenge grant and would reduce her taxable estate as well.

As Frank P. Wendt, retired chairman of John Nuveen &

Co., Inc., one of the country's oldest and largest investment bankers, is fond of saying, "People give primarily because an institution has benefited them personally, or they are motivated by its aspirations." Providing your donors with personal information on how they can benefit from giving can reap results even after many years of gift inactivity. Applying the five C's of major planned gift fund development will keep your supporters informed of your institution's aspirations. As donors age and give differently, a planned giving program may help secure more resources from this growing group than ever before. The results are gift plans that provide older individuals with the satisfaction and pleasure of continuing to see their charitable wishes fulfilled.

The Charitable Gift Annuity: Useful Instrument in the Planned Giving Toolbox

Richard Eppinga

Large institutions with established development offices may consider the charitable gift annuity a relatively unprofitable pursuit—too simple, suitable only for "mom-and-pop" operations, and not worth the trouble in comparison to trusts.

But sometimes the simplest solution is also the best. And "little people" deserve service too. Some of them, upon further examination, turn out to be not so little after all. And charitable gift annuities can be worthy of attention if trusts are beyond our expertise (they are for me) or if others can do the trusts for us (as is the case with me).

Small institutions with one-person advancement offices may believe they do not have the time or expertise to offer the charitable gift annuity. But, comparatively speaking, charitable gift annuities do not require much time to establish or much expertise and experience to offer. There are many situations in which the charitable gift annuity can prove mutually rewarding to donor and institution.

Calvin Theological Seminary in Grand Rapids, Michigan, is the seminary of the Christian Reformed Church in North America, a denomination of 300,000 members. It has 225 students and a budget of $2.9 million. My secretary and I constitute the advancement office.

In 1993 we wrote ten charitable gift annuities for $141,000. Two couples each established two contracts during the year. The smallest was $2,000; the largest was $60,000. Additionally we referred numerous people desiring anonymity in giving to an organization called the Barnabas Foundation that serves our denomination with professional planned giving and estate planning expertise. The Barnabas Foundation established $175,000 in charitable gift annuities for Calvin Seminary in addition to other estate work for us. Thus, we wrote charitable gift annuity contracts equivalent to almost five percent of our budget—more than ten percent with the assistance of the Barnabas Foundation. Considering that our seminary needs these gifts, that planned giving is the most easily postponed portion of my job, and that most of these charitable gift annuities sold themselves, I judge our efforts with charitable gift annuities to be well-spent.

What is a charitable gift annuity? It is a contract between an individual (or individuals) and a qualified charity that exchanges a gift to the charity for an annuity to the individual. What's an annuity? Guaranteed lifelong income; income one cannot outlive.

Charitable gift annuities offer donors many advantages, some of which are listed below, despite the risks of oversimplification in this short article:

Lifelong income, a portion of which is tax-exempt for a stated number of years.

Charitable income tax deduction when the annuity is established. If that deduction is larger than can be used in the year of the gift, the unused portion can be carried over for up to five years.

Exclusion from the estate for estate tax and inheritance tax purposes.

Attractive rate of interest—sometimes more than double the rate of any certificates of deposit (the greater the donor's age, the higher the rate of interest).

Dependable fixed rate of return.

Lifelong income for second person such as spouse or sibling.

Purchase with an appreciated asset as well as with cash, thus avoiding immediate payment of capital gains taxes and spreading payment over time.

Possible provision of income without disqualification

from Medicaid benefits.

Security of institutional assets standing behind annuity.

Not least, the satisfaction of making a significant gift to a loved cause.

Nothing on earth is perfect, including the charitable gift annuity. There are some limitations:

Irrevocability. Once given, the gift cannot be returned, no matter how compelling the need.

Vulnerability to inflation of the fixed rate of return.

Thirty-six month "look-back" period for "divestment-of-assets" test for Medicaid eligibility.

Some of the above apply to charitable gift annuities in Canada and some do not. Chief among the differences are the following:

Tax-exempt portion of charitable gift annuity income higher in Canada.

Tax-exempt portion of charitable gift income for the entire life of the donor in Canada, not just for the donor's actuarial life expectancy.

Higher rate of return in Canada.

Typical non-issuance of receipt for charitable contribution for the purposes of Revenue Canada.

Lower limit for charitable deductions in Canada.

Intermittent investigation by some provincial governments into which institutions may offer charitable gift annuities.

The ideal donors have presented themselves—an older couple in good health and not so much concerned with the principal of their life savings as with the amount of income they must derive from it. The following information should be obtained from them:

dates of birth, documentation,

amount of gift,

type of gift—cash or appreciated asset,

desired payment start date—immediate or deferred,

interval of payment—monthly, quarterly, semiannually, or annually.

It is best if the donors fill out and sign an application form. Additionally, when the charitable gift annuity is established, the donors also fill out a W-9 withholding form.

With the information above, the vital statistics of the charitable gift annuity can be generated by the institution's specialized computer software program, by a planned giving consultant or anyone else with the necessary computer resources, or by a vendor such as a life insurance company. Calvin Seminary receives the data from the Barnabas Foundation via a fax machine, usually within a half-hour of a telephone request.

With the data, Calvin Seminary prepares the following documents for the donors:

forms containing all the gift and annuity information,

cover letters to the annuitants reviewing the information above on an item-by-item basis,

charitable gift annuity agreements signed and witnessed by seminary personnel for the annuitants' files.

The following optional documents are appreciated by the annuitants: income tax reporting instructions (reporting is simple) and three pieces the annuitants will submit with their next federal income tax form—memo to the Internal Revenue Service reporting the establishment of the charitable gift annuity, copy of the signed charitable gift annuity agreement, and a copy of the charitable gift annuity information form.

What next? There are two possible courses of action. First, the advancement officer can deliver the donors' checks and a copy of the paperwork to the institution's investment officer, who invests and manages the money, sees to it that the donors receive their checks on time, and sends the donors a 1099 form each year for tax purposes. The gift does not appear on the annual budget gift income line until the donors die. At that time the institution will decide what to do with whatever is the then-current value of the gift.

This is the procedure followed by Calvin Seminary. The investment officer pools the gift with other monies, manages it actively and successfully, and generates the periodic reports on how the income pool is doing and how each individual piece of the pool is prospering.

Second, there is another course of action for institutions that cannot, or do not wish to, manage the charitable gift annuity. With the "annuity value" portion of the gift, the advancement officer purchases an annuity from a commercial vendor, usually an insurance company, and places the "gift value" of the annuity into the income stream for institutional allocation. The commercial vendor then mails the periodic checks to the annuitants and provides annual tax-reporting information.

Calvin Seminary is happy with the institutional management option. The gift income has been managed so well that, collectively speaking, when annuitants die and their annuities mature, the seminary receives not just the "gift value," but a sum that exceeds the amount of the initial gift, even after lifelong income has been paid.

Chapter Five:
Major Gift Fund Raising

How to Build
a Major Gifts Program

David Heetland

Development officers are fond of saying that there are three irrefutable rules which assure your success as a fund raiser. Unfortunately no one has ever discovered what they are! I do not claim to have discovered these rules. However, I have discovered three principles, originally articulated by G. T. Smith, president emeritus of Chapman College, which have served me well in building a major gifts program.

1. Development is a very simple business. We really have only two goals: 1) to create an understanding of the mission, values, and accomplishments of an institution, and 2) to secure the necessary support in goodwill and dollars to sustain and advance the institution.

2. Development is much more than simply concern for money. In fact, fund raising is more spiritual than financial. The primary focus of development is the human spirit and its aspirations.

3. Most gift support should and usually will come from those closest to the institution, normally trustees, alums, and close friends. A relatively small number of people, ranging from a half dozen to a hundred, will make the critical difference in nearly every institution.

It follows from these three principles that the single most important function in a successful development program is the cultivation of major gifts. A former development guideline stated that eighty percent of the money would come from twenty percent of the donors. Today we recognize that this is an understatement, and it is not unusual for ninety percent or more of the money to come from ten percent of the donors. Since ninety percent or more of total giving comes from major gifts, a proportionate share of our development resources (staff, time, and budget) should be allocated accordingly.

What is a major gift? Gerald J. Brock, development consultant, writes:

> *Basically major gifts are those gifts which play*
> *a major role in reaching the fund raising goal.*
> *Using the rule of thumb that says "In most*
> *successful fund raising efforts, the top gift is*
> *ten percent to fifteen percent of the goal, the top*
> *ten gifts are equal to approximately forty percent*
> *of the goal, and the top one hundred gifts will be*
> *responsible for ninety percent of what is raised,"*
> *a simple definition of major gifts then becomes*
> *"the top one hundred prospects."*

My own institution's experience closely parallels the above figures. In July 1988 we completed a campaign which resulted in commitments totaling $10.4 million. The top gift represented nineteen percent of the goal, the top ten gifts represented fifty-four percent of the goal, and the top one hundred gifts represented eighty-nine percent of the goal.

We were so impressed by these statistics which revealed the critical importance of major gifts that following the campaign we implemented a program to identify, inform, and involve our top one hundred prospects. Today we have our top one hundred prospects (our "major" prospects) on one of three lists: our top ten, the next twenty, the final seventy. These lists are reviewed monthly by staff and volunteers, and cultivation steps are planned and noted beside each name. As contacts are actually made, this information is added to the lists. The top ten get the most attention—usually from the president and a key volunteer. The next twenty are my major responsibility, and the cultivation for the rest is usually coordinated by other development staff. These lists are fluid, with names continually being moved up or down or off the lists entirely.

This relatively simple process of maintaining and reviewing these lists has helped our development staff, our president, and our volunteers to keep focused on the identification and cultivation of major gift prospects as a top priority. It serves to remind us that there is no magic or mystery in major gift solicitation. It simply takes a lot of hard work, honest caring, and a belief in the cause we represent.

The steps in obtaining major gifts are often described as prospect identification, cultivation, solicitation, and recognition. Perhaps an easier way to remember the steps is to think of the four R's: research, romance, request, and recognition. Ernest W. Wood, vice president of the Russ Reid Company, suggests that "major gift solicitation is about twenty-five percent research, sixty percent romance, five percent request, and ten percent recognition." What he terms romance, of course, is simply those continuing contacts (dates, if you will) designed to bring a person closer to an institution. Reid's emphasis on romance is a good reminder that asking someone with money but no relationship to an institution for a major gift is as foolhardy as asking an attractive stranger to marry you just because you think he or she is eligible.

I personally find G. T. Smith's five steps to securing major gifts the most helpful. His five steps all begin with the letter "I":

Identification—identifying those who could be major gift supporters. Remember, the likelihood is that they are the ones closest to your institution. In our campaign, for example, the largest gift commitment came from a trustee. The second largest commitment came from an alum, and the third largest commitment came from a former faculty member.

Information—learning additional information about the potential donor. This is the "research" step, where the "researcher" comes to know a whole person with individual tastes, values, and interests, rather than just a potential donor. Some of the best research takes place not in county courthouses or public libraries, but in face-to-face visits with prospective friends.

Interest—furthering the prospect's interests. Successful

organizations offer donors opportunities not only to meet the needs of others, but to find personal fulfillment at the same time. Giving, whether it be of time, talent, or treasure, should provide opportunities for donors to pursue an interest, fulfill a dream, or leave a mark in the world. In our campaign we were fortunate to be able to provide meaningful, challenging work to an individual at the time of his retirement by making him campaign chair. His wife thanked us on several occasions for giving him something meaningful to do, and we were rewarded many times over by having a capable, enthusiastic volunteer donating hundreds of hours of time.

Involvement—encouraging meaningful involvement. When the interests of the individual are creatively matched with the goals of the organization, meaningful involvement results. The greater the involvement, the greater the likelihood of increased gifts, for institutions are developing loyal and faithful supporters who respond out of their total being. One of our trustees once confided to a faculty member that he was considering resigning from the board until he was asked to chair a task force which more appropriately utilized his gifts. Not surprisingly, his financial support also increased.

Investment—receiving added financial investment. If persons have been appropriately identified, informed, and involved in ways that are of interest to them, there is a good probability that they also will be willing to invest their financial resources generously. Persons tend to invest the most charitable dollars where they also invest their time and talent.

Sometimes interest and involvement are so high that people will take the initiative in making substantial gifts without even being asked. There is a marvelous story about a university president who was well known for his fund raising successes. When asked for the reason, the president's reply was that he never asked for money. Rather, he would take potential donors on a tour of the campus and share with them his dreams. Time after time persons with resources would help make those dreams a reality. In addition to sharing his dreams, this president was obviously savvy enough to do his homework and make sure his dreams coincided with potential donor interests. His approach also provided persons with opportunities, not desperate needs.

The president's method may well sound like the ideal situation, but fund raising doesn't always happen that way! When it doesn't come so easily, which will probably be the majority of the time, we must not forget to invite persons to make an investment of their financial resources. We cannot lose sight of the fact that securing a gift is the hoped for end of this whole process.

These five steps (identification, information, interest, involvement, and investment) should comprise a continuing cycle as we seek to develop and nurture persons who are involved and committed to our mission. A significant portion of our development effort should be directed toward leading our major gift prospects through these five steps. If we can remember this, and consistently practice this, we will be well on our way to a strong major gifts program.

Ministry Sundays

Don R. Locher

For many years our school promoted a program entitled "STC Sundays." The president and other representatives of the School of Theology at Claremont went to churches to seek support. Sometimes this meant preaching, sometimes speaking at scheduled luncheons, and sometimes only a brief promotional time during the worship service. The seminary's message gradually became one of constant financial crisis. These events became increasingly less popular and more difficult to schedule. In July 1992, we changed focus. We initiated Ministry Sundays. The idea, which is disarmingly simple, has found enthusiastic reception. We emphasize our gratitude for ministry by honoring our alums instead of emphasizing our needs. We work with local churches in celebrating pastoral anniversaries and retirements.

We recognized that most pastors seldom, if ever, receive a well-planned corporate expression of gratitude. We determined that one function of our seminary could be to publicly recognize, with appreciation, those ministries that reflect most fully the kind of theological education and preparation we have provided. In specifically honoring a beloved pastor as a distinguished alum, we lift up the whole profession of ministry. Whenever possible, we initiate a named scholarship as a most appropriate way to honor a ministry. This option is always offered, but is not necessary to celebrate a Ministry Sunday.

The president, or someone on our faculty selected by the pastor being honored, is usually the preacher. We ask for ten minutes in the service to make our presentation. Often a special reception or luncheon follows worship. In most cases we establish, with the pastor's consent, a named scholarship. We open and place the first $1,000 in the named fund within our endowment. When other interested persons bring the endowment account to

$15,000 the (pastor's name) scholarship will provide $1,000 per year to a deserving student.

Since we began this program, I have contacted thirty-two pastors. Only one was not interested at the time. The other thirty-one pastors enthusiastically scheduled a Ministry Sunday. We are now beginning to receive requests.

What have we learned? Ministry Sundays work best when the pastor provides names of leaders and potential organizers for a local committee to plan the celebration. Phone conversations are generally sufficient to motivate and resource the committee. It is better when I meet with the committee in their initial organization and better yet when we have a second meeting.

Ministry Sundays work best when we honor a very effective pastor in good standing on the occasion of a tenth, twentieth, twenty-fifth, thirtieth, or fortieth anniversary. When the pastor's previous pastorates are invited to send representatives or letters to the celebration the events grow in significance.

Some donors to the named scholarship fund work for matching gift companies. This greatly strengthens the local church committee's motivation to build the scholarship.

Ministry Sundays demonstrate that our seminary is an agency of service with a continuing interest in our graduates. This is providing our churches and pastors with a more positive view of our seminary. Other positive by-products of Ministry Sundays include discovering potential members for our seminary advisory board and developing a growing list of possible donors.

Our Ministry Sundays program is still evolving. Research into anniversaries and retirements of our alums has provided more than enough possibilities for the next two years, and we are also considering honoring persons other than local church pastors. We believe the program is best served with a low profile, so we do not normally publish names of those honored.

Giving Real Estate

Frank A. Mullen

While planning for charitable giving has become increasingly sophisticated over the years, one form of gift remains simple and effective: a gift of real estate. Real estate is an asset donors do not always consider as they plan their gifts. It is, however, an excellent way to make a gift to your seminary, for a gift of real estate helps enhance the seminary's activities and programs while offering substantial tax benefits and philanthropic satisfaction to donors.

The following are some ways real estate can be given:

Outright gift. An outright gift is the simplest way of making a gift of real estate. Like other forms of giving, the outright gift of real estate may be designated for a specific purpose that the donor may find of particular interest. It may also remain unrestricted, used to help defray the seminary's general educational expenses.

When the donor makes an outright gift of real estate, the seminary retains ownership of the property and uses it for its educational or administrative needs.

Whether the institution keeps or sells the property, the donor will receive an income tax charitable deduction based upon full market value of the property, not its original cost. Because there will be no capital gains or estate tax implications, the donor will be able to make a gift larger and more beneficial than a direct gift of cash.

Life income gift. By giving real estate in trust to an institution, the donor can receive an annual income of a minimum of five percent of the fair market value of the trust assets. It is likely that the trustee, often the institution, will sell the real estate and invest the proceeds. Annual income from those proceeds in trust will be based on a percentage of the assets, decided by the donor at the time he or she creates the trust. There may be tax savings on this annual income as well. Once the lifetime interests in the trust expire, the institution will receive the trust assets.

Generally, this gift plan is established through a charitable remainder unitrust, though other life income plans are also available. For example, a donor could fund a pooled income fund or a charitable gift annuity through a real estate gift. All have a special appeal to donors whose real estate has appreciated over the years.

Gift with retention of lifetime use. If a donor owns a personal residence, a vacation home, or a farm that he or she has considered giving through a provision in a will, he or she may be able to arrange for your institution to receive property in the future while the donor retains life use of the property for himself and for another beneficiary.

This type of arrangement is called a gift of residence or farm with retained life estate. Like a bequest, it provides a substantial or even a complete reduction of federal estate taxes on the property. But, unlike a bequest, it offers an immediate charitable tax deduction.

Bargain sale gift. If a donor wants to give real estate but does not feel able to make a gift of the property's total value, he or she may transfer the property by means of a bargain sale. In a bargain sale, which is part gift and part sale, the seminary buys the property from him for a price less than its fair market value. The difference between the property's fair market value and the purchase price paid is considered a gift for which he or she is entitled to claim a charitable tax deduction. Because he or she receives both sales proceeds and the income tax charitable deduction, the total return in most instances will be only slightly less than what he or she would have received on the sale of the property at fair market value.

Gift of undivided interest in property. A donor may also consider giving only a portion of his or her ownership. Called an undivided interest, such a gift may be any fractional share of the whole property.

For example, a donor could give a one-half undivided interest in his or her real estate, retaining the other one-half interest and claim an income tax charitable deduction for the full fair market value of one-half of the property.

Gift by bequest. Although there are many innovative ways of making charitable gifts, most seminaries still rely on bequests for most of their endowment financial support. While life income gifts with retention of lifetime use can offer financial benefits not offered by a bequest, many people, for a number of sound financial and philanthropic reasons, prefer to make their gifts by bequest. The bequest of real estate is an excellent way to make a gift.

There are a number of ways to make a bequest of real estate. Choices include bequests which are outright, residuary, contingent, or in trust. All offer the donor the opportunity to make a gift while assuring the financial well-being of his or her family.

Be careful of swamps in Georgia (check for alligators) and oil wells in Oklahoma (look for old rigs); otherwise, go ahead and accept the real estate. The donor must pay for a qualified appraisal, not demand unreasonable restrictions, and sometimes (if needed) pay for legal fees. Make sure your seminary really wants the old farmhouse, garage, or cornfield before you get too involved.

Reflections on a Capital Campaign: What's Most Important?

David Heetland

When Garrett-Evangelical Theological Seminary formally launched a capital campaign in October 1986, the seminary's goal was to raise $8.3 million for endowment and capital improvements. My personal goal was to learn something in the process. With approximately $1 million yet to raise, it looks promising that the seminary's goal will soon be realized. My personal goal already has been realized many times over! The following are what I would suggest as the most important keys to a capital campaign:

Feasibility studies. We knew our goals were important. We knew our key friends supported these goals. We had been discussing a campaign for years, it seemed. Was a feasibility study really necessary? I am convinced more than ever that feasibility studies are essential prior to embarking on a major campaign. The feasibility study validated our goals. It also revealed that we needed to do a better job of "telling our story" to a wider group of people. Perhaps most importantly, it helped "set the stage" for launching the campaign by creating a mood of expectancy among our key leaders.

Case statement. The case statement can take many forms: a simple typed document, a professionally printed brochure complete with pictures, an audiovisual. We used many forms at various times during the campaign and have found each helpful with particular constituencies. The typed document worked well with key leaders familiar with the seminary in the initial stages of the campaign, the audiovisual was especially helpful in group settings, and the professional brochure was a good introduction of the seminary to folks unfamiliar with the institution. In each form, simplicity was the key word.

Support of key leaders. There is no use attempting a campaign unless the trustees and the administration wholeheartedly support it with their time and their finances. We have been very fortunate to have a campaign chair who has enthusiastically given tremendous amounts of time talking about the seminary to individuals and small groups across the country. Equally important has been the willingness of our president to devote up to fifty percent of his time to the development effort. Other trustees, faculty, and administrators have also given of their time when called upon. Virtually one hundred percent participation by trustees and faculty in making campaign pledges at the beginning also set the pace for the campaign.

Outside counsel. In regard to outside counsel someone once remarked, "You can't live with them, and you can't live without them." Though outside counsel is never inexpensive, I prefer to live with them for several reasons: they bring a depth of experience from other campaigns, they keep the development staff and president focused on campaign goals, and they can often say things to key leaders that need to be said but may not be heard if said by one of the development staff. The amount of outside counsel needed depends on how much campaign experience the president, staff, and trustees have, and whether or not they plan to expand the development staff during the campaign.

Alums. We sold ourselves short on our alums! While the vast majority of our graduates are not wealthy, we initially failed to recognize just how important they can be. Many alums are instrumental in introducing leadership donors to the seminary. When we discovered this fact we readjusted our timeline to contact all alums earlier in the campaign. Another happy surprise was discovering how generous alums can be when they believe in a campaign. Our original alum goal was $770,000. To date they have pledged well over a million dollars!

Flexibility. In addition to changing the campaign timetable we have changed the campaign goal (from $8.3 million to $8.5 million), the time commitment of our outside counsel, and indeed our campaign strategy at several points. I believe such flexibility has played a key role in our success to date, and would stress the importance of hiring campaign counsel who are willing to be flexible.

Foundation support. While many foundations may not be interested in supporting theological education, a few are, and their support can make a significant difference in the overall campaign goal. Foundations should not be overlooked, particularly if the campaign has a "bricks and mortar" component. While our original goal for foundations was $200,000, we now hope to surpass $1 million in foundation support.

Planned gifts. The debate continues as to whether or not planned gifts should be counted toward campaign goals. We made the decision to count planned gift commitments from persons sixty years of age or older. This has enabled alums and others to make more significant gifts than otherwise possible, and has opened the door for long-term cultivation of these persons. A happy by-product of counting planned gifts has been that several persons, after making a planned gift commitment, have decided to give the gift now instead!

The annual fund. In the midst of a capital campaign it is very easy to lose sight of the annual fund. We have tried to have a separate annual fund campaign with an increased goal from previous years at the same time that we were devoting ninety percent of our time to the capital campaign—and it didn't work! If I were to do it over again, I would incorporate the annual fund and capital campaign requests into one. It is too confusing to most people to keep straight fiscal years, campaign pledges, and annual fund pledges—and many didn't.

A sense of humor. How else can you respond— and still keep your sanity — when someone makes a $10 gift and requests that it be divided among three funds, or when the person who expresses a wish to make a million dollar gift in the feasibility study fails to make a pledge, or when. . . .

Chapter Six:
Working With Other Professionals

A Guide for
Administrative Assistants

Delora A. Roop

When I entered the position of administrative assistant, I never suspected the job could be so varied. At some time or other you may find yourself being everything from a custodian picking up after a reception to a development colleague helping plan strategy for an upcoming fund raising campaign.

The position of administrative assistant calls for flexibility, support, and attention to detail. Consider some suggestions for fine tuning the work:

You are an assistant. It is crucial for you to be available to others to assist them in carrying out their tasks. You may find yourself helping the secretary seal envelopes or assisting the director of development to prepare the CASE/CFAE report. Your job is to assist.

Be prepared to drop everything. A couple on vacation decided to stop for a tour of the seminary. They did not call ahead but arrived unexpectedly. The receptionist phoned me to say that the visitors would like a tour. At that point I had to drop everything and arrange for the tour. There is never a second chance for the seminary to make a first impression.

Acknowledge gifts promptly. Design systems so that a donor receives a thank you note and receipt in the shortest possible time—perhaps even the same day. A prompt reply reinforces good feelings about the gift. Perhaps the acknowledgment letter becomes "old hat" to those of us responsible for getting them out, but it is likely a very serious link and a lasting impression to the donor who receives it.

Keep track of names. Be a detective—take initiative for tracking down changes in names, addresses, or phone numbers. Scan church newsletters, local newspapers, and correspondence for any changes you can use on your data base. If you spot any significant change in the life of a donor, make sure that the director of development knows about it.

Record sources of information. It is difficult to remember from one year to the next the source of the figures needed for various annual reports. To remedy this problem, make notes in the margins of the copy you retain for your files, identifying how and where you obtained the figures for that report.

Design reminder systems to help you (and others) remember that the board report is due on October 20 or that the director of development needs to follow up with a donor in three weeks. One of the most valuable services you can offer is to manage the "tickler" system for the office staff.

Prioritize mail for those you assist. Date and stamp each item. Then, organize the most important mail into different stacks or by putting the most important on top. You can save others incredible amounts of time by the way you open, note, and organize their mail.

File by common sense. Set up the files with labels that mean something to you and to others in the office. Think about how one would normally classify an item. For example, in setting up a file for rental cars, would you look first for Rental Vehicles, Car Rental, or Auto Rental? Here's a tip: when in doubt, file under the same headings as the phone book. Rental cars are under Automobile Renting. Attorneys are listed under Lawyers. On your file label, underline the letter of the word you use for filing.

Maintain confidentiality. You are a trusted staff member with a wealth of confidential information at your fingertips. Such information is not yours to release. Maintain the highest personal standards of confidentiality. If you are working with confidential papers and need to leave the office, put the papers out of sight and clear the information from your computer screen.

The Development Office
and the Business Office:
Learning How to Work Together

John J.M. O'Brien Prager

The development office and the business office are both concerned about the seminary's financial health. However, they have different procedures, priorities, and responsibilities. Here are several areas where approaches differ.

Accounting periods. They are seldom the same. The business office may use a June 30 fiscal year (most schools do), and development may use a calendar year. If development uses an academic or fiscal year, individuals often are confused about which campaign they supported. Development should use the accounting period that is easiest for the seminary's donors. A calendar year matches most individual giving habits and tax years. Development and business office reports must be reconciled and differences clarified.

Fund accounting. Nearly all schools use fund accounting principles. A good analysis is contained in *Management Reporting Standards for Educational Institutions: Fund Raising and Related Activities* by the Council for Advancement and Support of Education (CASE) and the National Association of College and University Business Officers (NACUBO).

Even when guidelines are followed, business and development reports differ. If you doubt that, try to complete an ATS or CASE financial statement from a business office report. It can't be done. There are two reasons:

First, the business office deals with revenues and expenditures, the development office with sources. To budget and monitor expenditures, the business office looks at the amount in and purpose of a fund. Source is immaterial. The development office wants to know fund source for donor tracking and reporting.

Second, business and development accounts have different totals. The business office includes interest and realized capital gain and probably covers a different fiscal year. Account integrity is critical, because the business office segregates funds for use but commingles them for investment.

Financial accuracy. It is the business office's responsibility. The seminary has one official financial statement—the business office's. The auditors use it for their report. To maintain business office record integrity, the development office does not access business records (not even "read only"). Development requests specific information from the business office when needed.

Should business and development maintain their own data bases on a central computer (it is not practical to have one financial data base because of account integrity), or should development have its own, stand-alone system? When the number of donors is small and it is cost effective to acquire personal computer programs and hardware, a stand-alone development system works (although account reconciliation is more difficult). For larger operations, however, development and business offices should use separate, cross-linked bases on a networked system to ensure central control of data entry and transfer. Either way, be prepared for program revision and fine tuning—it is a constant process. Moses got the only set of in-stone commands.

Development inputs all donative data. The business office does not enter gifts. Development daily submits a computer-generated transmittal form and all checks to the business office. The form contains all pertinent information (e.g., donor identification number, gift amount, account code/purpose) with supportive documentation when needed. Original wills, annuities, insurance policies, and deeds should be kept in a central depository, usually the business office. The business office verifies entry accuracy. Business office determinations govern. If a change is required, the business office requests development to submit a revised transmittal form. If the figures are correct, the

157

business office approves the entries for development and business records. Development and business entries are reconciled and entered into their respective systems by the close of business.

Account management. Management of pooled income, annuity and trust accounts is time-consuming. If the number of accounts is large, too much business office effort is consumed. While supervising all investments, the business office may delegate disbursement tasks to an independent firm. Development responsibility technically ends when the gift is accepted, but it is prudent periodically to check with the business office to ensure that problems have not arisen with any donor's account.

Tax law considerations. Development reports relevant tax changes to the business office and suggests appropriate action. An easy example is the 1991 revised mileage allowance. A more complicated case is the recent IRS ruling that a pooled income fund must have a depreciation reserve if depreciable property is accepted as a gift. Development works with the business and legal counsel to ensure IRS compliance.

Unrelated business income—renting space for commercial purposes like a concert—is an issue for the business office. Be aware of the situation, since it may involve development in local business concerns.

Acceptable donated property. Development enthusiasm to complete a gift for institutional advancement must be balanced by sound business practice. The business office determines the type of real and personal property that the seminary will accept. Securities that do not meet the institution's investment policy (e.g., a company doing business in South Africa) are liquidated. Acceptance of stock in a closely held or family business may appear beneficial both to the donor and the seminary, but the securities may prove to be overvalued, unsalable, or, if held, embroil the institution in costly intrafamilial litigation. Careful background checks are essential.

The business office may not want to become an absentee landlord struggling to manage property throughout the country. Liability exposure is great. Horror stories abound of a school accepting property from a seemingly well-intended donor, only to discover that the transferred property consists of substandard housing or a structure requiring extensive maintenance that no longer can be deferred.

Environmental concerns pose additional problems. The New Jersey Supreme Court, in a recent landmark ruling, expanded the scope of liability of the owner of contaminated property. A seemingly well-sited tract of land can become an institution's "Love Canal." The fact that the seminary is a nonprofit, good-faith donee of the property does not relieve it of the liability and expense to clean up the mess. Legal action against the donor may be impractical, expensive, or futile.

Special event liability. Normally a business office responsibility, development must be aware of insurance policy scope. If development invites a local congregation to tour the campus, are invitees automatically covered, or must the business office obtain special rider coverage? What if the congregation invites itself? Is there a difference between a visiting congregation and a church youth group using the seminary's gym for a basketball game? What about a seminary-sponsored athletic event open to the general public, like a mini-marathon to support a local soup kitchen?

Development wants to help without imposing any burden on a church or youth group. The business office, however, may insist that a church carry (and provide proof of) its own insurance plus indemnification of the seminary if a church member or youth participant is injured. The seminary can lose public good will and expose itself to extensive liability if the business and development offices fail to work together.

Consultants and equipment. Spend money to raise money. Development wants to; the business office may not. Standard objections are: Why use consultants? Doesn't development know what it's doing? Are new, expensive computers cost-effective?

Do as much in-house as possible. Administrative expenses are a concern for the seminary and its donors. To train new staff or initiate a campaign, however, a consultant may be essential as well as cost-effective. Even a successful development office warrants periodic review by an outside expert.

Low overhead is good stewardship. But not every development operation shows up on a balance sheet. The free alum magazine and the time spent on class reunions are important, even if they are not evidenced on the business office's credit ledger.

Develop a team approach to money. Development's best friend is the business office. Approaches vary, but the goal is the same: the seminary's financial viability. An icon of Jesus washing his disciples' feet hangs in my office. It reminds me what *vocatio* really means for both the development office and the business office.

Helping Faculty Find Funds

Cheryl Tupper

The Graduate Theological Union (GTU) in Berkeley established a grants office devoted to funding the research and scholarship of theological faculty. The office, funded by a grant from the Lilly Endowment serves two purposes: 1) provide grant seeking assistance to the 150 faculty members of the GTU consortial schools, and 2) develop resources and a model of a faculty grants office for member institutions of ATS.

Although most faculty projects fall within the rubric of the humanities, few seminary faculty members have actively sought grants from humanities organizations. There are a couple of factors which contribute to this. Unlike their counterparts in other disciplines, theological faculty members have not been dependent on grants and contracts for support of their research and resulting scholarship. In the past the small costs of research and writing have been able to be absorbed by the institution or individual; consequently there was no great motivation to seek external funding. As a result of this, organizations that fund humanities research are not well acquainted with theological scholarship.

Nationally, there are only three funding sources that give non-programmatic fellowship grants to scholars in the humanities: the American Council of Learned Societies (ACLS), the National Endowment for the Humanities (NEH), and the John Simon Guggenheim Foundation. This signals the highly competitive nature of these grants which can make it difficult to convince a faculty member that all of the time and effort needed to write a grant proposal will be worthwhile. The funding ratio for the number of applicants to fellowship granted is ACLS 14:1, Guggenheim 12:1, and NEH 6:1.

There are certainly other funding sources available to faculty, most of which are either program-specific, residential, or both. Program-specific means that the faculty member's research has to fall within the specific program interests of the organization such as women's studies, Byzantine history, biomedical ethics, et cetera. Residential fellowships require that the scholar be located at a particular institution and often require teaching or participation in seminars in addition to research.

Faculty who are interested in applying for individual grants may find the following suggestions helpful:

Tips for Faculty

Call first. Talking with program officers in advance of submitting a proposal is highly recommended since they can advise you as to whether or not the project sounds appropriate and fundable. This can prevent needless disappointment and save hours of intense work. If your project doesn't fit their priorities, they will tell you. Program officers will sometimes offer tips on the best way to complete the application and may supply information that is helpful in focusing your project.

Allow adequate lead time. Planning for sabbatical funding should begin at least one-and-a-half years before the leave begins. It frequently takes a scholar that amount of time to fine tune a project to the degree necessary to write a good grant proposal. Since grant deadlines vary, adequate lead time will also safeguard against missing any particular grant cycle.

Outline the facts. When are funds needed? What is the nature of the proposed study? How much money is required and for what purpose (make budget drafts along the way)? Where will you be located and what, if any, travel is involved?

Research funding sources. Get help from your seminary's development officers to identify sources and strategies for funding. Development officers can point the way to directories, the Foundation Library and its programs, and possible contacts. The faculty member should do the preliminary homework of writing for annual reports, applications, and prospecti.

Prepare the application or proposal. Preparing the application materials is the faculty member's responsibility. However, development officers have written countless proposals and might offer to review the application or proposal in light of their experience.

Write clearly. Program officers at foundations say that the most common reason a proposal gets rejected is that the proposed project is not clear. Avoid jargon or technical language.

Specify the outcome. What are you going to do and what will be the tangible outcomes? Don't get bogged down in the background, history, and intellectual substance of the project. Clearly state the anticipated outcome of the work. It is extremely important to make a persuasive argument for why a project is important and why you should be the one to do it.

Consider collaboration. Collaborative projects among faculty can be more fundable than individual projects. Some foundations state in the guidelines that they prefer collaborative research.

Look for interdisciplinary links. Another way to increase a project's funding potential is to expand its interdisciplinary links. Many of the residential programs prefer that a faculty member's research draw on more than one field within the humanities or the social sciences.

Be open and flexible. It is often the more obscure, little-known organizations that will be interested in a proposed project.

Keep trying. Development officers know from experience: sometimes you don't get a grant the first time you apply. Don't take rejections personally—it's very competitive. Try again, and try more than one funding source.

Development Officers
and Stewardship Education

David Mertz

Recently, as one of two development officers in a room full of theological educators, I attended a colloquy on steward-ship education sponsored by the Ecumenical Center for Stewardship Studies (ECSS). Expenses were covered by ECSS with only one condition—that each attendee offer a course on stewardship at his or her own institution during the next two years.

That ECSS was willing to fly me and eighteen others to Waterloo, Canada, and provide us with room, board, and three days of instruction and conversation started me to think back on my own education regarding stewardship. Basically, I learned about stewardship the way many learn about sex—by trial and error, and without much formal education.

Since most pastors and professors know that Jesus talked about money more often than he did prayer, it is reasonable to ask the two-part question, "Why is stewardship so neglected in theo-logical education, and why is it such an uncomfortable topic for so many in the church—clergy and laity alike?" In offering some reasons for reluctance, let me begin with seminaries.

Stewardship courses, and by association those who teach them, often are considered peripheral. It is a rare student who views a stewardship course with the same awe as he or she views a Greek New Testament course. Stewardship educators (and development officers) are often seen as people who for whatever reason could not make it in the church, or could not get a "real" PhD. The implication of this is that academia sees stewardship education as a low priority and someone else's responsibility.

Another possibility is that the body/spirit dualism is alive and well in both the academy and the church, and money, of course, deals with the body. Hence, those who deal with it are held in lower esteem than are those who deal with matters of the mind. The reality, of course, is that money is fundamentally a spiritual issue.

Thus, the Horizon Research study (presented at the DIAP gathering in February 1992) should come as no great surprise. This study showed that more than eighty percent of practicing clergy thought it was important for seminaries to offer seminary or continuing education courses on stewardship, but fewer than five percent would be extremely interested in taking such a course.

I admit that in seminary I would have fit the research—thinking the material important, but only secondarily so, and certainly not wanting to take a course in it. Like many of us, I wanted to take advantage of classes in Bible, theology, and preaching, believing that the practical aspects of ministry would be learned in the field.

One possibility for churches' reluctance to address money in a straightforward fashion is that even after experience proves otherwise, many pastors continue to believe that if the preaching is good and the theology sound, the other stuff will fall into place, and the people will give.

Talking about money often turns to pastors' salaries, and pastors are reminded, both directly and indirectly, of their dependence on others.

No matter what the cause, people feel like they are begging when asking for money. The problem, again, is a poor understanding of stewardship and the role of money in one's spiritual development.

Other reasons include reaction to church scandals, embarrassment over so personal and sensitive an issue, and a simple lack of preparation for stewardship education.

Clearly, stewardship education is needed. Neither the seminary I attended nor the one at which I work offers it. None of the thirteen United Methodist seminaries I checked offers a course on stewardship, and only three include it as part of another regular course on church administration. As a pastor, I did learn a lot in the field, but not all of it was effective, well-organized, or even very useful. I had to do many things wrong before I understood that there was a better way.

A stewardship course has the possibility of integrating a great deal of theological education into one coherent whole. The course would be biblically based, theologically grounded, and practically oriented. A mission or social witness emphasis would be crucial.

Church institutions are getting more sophisticated about development. Seminaries now have development officers. Denominations are finding new ways to encourage churches to develop bequest and planned giving programs, and are hiring planned giving specialists. Many annual conferences of The United Methodist Church have established foundations (Northern New Jersey voted last year to establish one, with a $30 million goal by the year 2000), and I suspect other judicatories are doing the same. More churches are finding themselves with sudden endowments and the attendant opportunities and burdens they bring.

Churches deserve a more sophisticated, less apologetic approach that can help parishioners develop a sense of money as a spiritual issue—and hence one that can lead to spiritual growth. The only way a church can have such an approach is for its pastor to provide the requisite leadership.

In my untested assumption, the best student would be a third-year student who has gained the ability to integrate what he or she has learned; can see the theological implications of an assumption, position, or activity; has had some field work experience; and may have gone through a stewardship campaign or two. Another audience may be nearby pastors of various denominations who need a refresher course or who feel their skills are somewhat inadequate now that they have been "out there" for a while.

Such a course should be marketed to students, and not merely listed in the semester's course offerings. We have to be realistic that even though we are teaching this course, students may still prefer to spend their time in a Greek Bible course.

In another untested assumption, I think a spring semester, afternoon seminar, offered once a week for less than full-time credit would be the optimal arrangement. Thus, the course would not be in competition with other full-credit courses (or in competition with other faculty!), and might attract students who need one or two credits to graduate but who might not otherwise take a course on stewardship.

Why should a development officer teach it? We know something about it. We have the necessary theological foundation and practical experience.

We know pastors in the area whose stewardship has been effective and who would be honored to bring that experience into the classroom. Most pastors have gained some wisdom over the years and would appreciate the invitation to share that wisdom. This also strengthens the ties between the seminary and that pastor and church.

Teaching a course is an opportunity to become better acquainted with students and local pastors than development officers often have. We could help provide part of the bridge students cross when moving from seminary to full-time parish ministry. After graduation, we could be available as a contact and resource person. The course and continuing contact could strengthen alum ties and commitment to the institution over the years.

A semester-long classroom experience might help students (and faculty!) answer the often asked question of the development office: "What do those people do?" In my case, I was lucky: a faculty member with whom I work quite closely suggested I attend the ECSS colloquy and then teach the class. The dean was also quite supportive. Without his help, none of this would come to pass.

Finally, and most important, more pastors might develop more fully their own theology of giving, and then lead their churches on that same rewarding journey.

Few theological educators have chosen to take this mantle as their own. Clearly the church needs someone to take the lead, and we as development officers may be the right people at the right time.

Consultants:
What to Know Before You Sign

Billie J. Hooker

With the ever increasing competition for the philanthropic dollar, fund raising efforts have expanded and escalated in recent years. A wide range of nonprofit organizations regularly launch many different kinds of fund raising activities. It is the capital campaign, however, which remains the primary vehicle for seeking substantial sums of money to meet long-term organizational needs.

It is virtually unheard of for an organization to attempt a capital campaign without the benefit of professional counsel. Even when there is a full-time professional staff in place, it is unlikely that staff can manage the other essentials of an ongoing development program while addressing the rigors of a capital campaign. Among the distinct advantages brought by consultants are objectivity, broad experience from numerous capital campaigns, and ability to focus clearly and completely on the task.

The three most important functions of the consultant will be conducting the feasibility study, developing the case statement, and managing the campaign. Specific responsibilities of the consultant during the campaign include:

    analyzing the goals,
    devising record-keeping procedures,
    developing an organizational chart,
    establishing budget procedures,
    implementing reporting mechanisms,
    planning the sequence of activities,
    assisting with promotional materials,
    training staff and volunteers,
    ensuring the adherence to a timetable.

There are other less tangible but no less significant benefits of a consultant's involvement in a capital campaign. Counsel can serve as a sounding board for staff and can reinforce messages from staff to the administration and campaign leadership. The consultant is usually able to bypass the internal politics that frequently impede development efforts. Often consultants leave behind guidelines and blueprints for long-range development efforts, and almost always staff will have gained knowledge and expertise.

Great care must be exercised in choosing a consultant or consultant firm. Networking with other institutions can provide valuable leads and evaluation. Careful investigation of a firm's credentials and track record is essential.

Selecting counsel should be the task of a committee comprised of board members, the institution's chief executive officer, and the chief development officer. When none of these individuals has had experience with capital campaigns or consultants, it is wise to add someone to the committee who has.

Once choices have been narrowed, it is important to determine the following: Who runs the firm? What has been done with similar organizations and comparable goals? What exactly will the firm do and how? Who will be assigned to your campaign? What results are expected? How much will it cost?

When the consultant has been chosen and consensus is reached on the job to be done, the next step should be a written agreement or contract. The agreement should include the purpose of the assignment, the methodology, the product to be delivered, fees and expenses, methods of payment, timetables for beginning and ending the campaign, and designation of the firm's personnel who will conduct your campaign. Moreover, the agreement should indicate the provisions for terminating the consultant-client relationship if it becomes necessary. Vital elements for a harmonious, productive relationship with consultants include:

clarifying the roles of the consultant and the development staff,

providing adequate staff support for the consultant,

encouraging candor from the consultant,

monitoring the consultant's activities and conducting periodic evaluation sessions.

The emphasis through the entire process is on forging a workable team effort among the consultant, the development officer, and the volunteer leadership. A careful, deliberate process of planning and selection is key to ensuring a mutually beneficial association and a successful capital campaign.

Development Officers and Lawyers

Ray Caraway

In what ways should development officers be concerned about intruding into the realm rightfully reserved for lawyers? What role should development officers play in helping donors obtain the best possible legal advice? What type of contact should development officers have with donors' attorneys? I hope the following discussion will shed some light on these issues and encourage all of us to contemplate how we can best serve the interest of our donors.

The mention of unauthorized practice of law may bring to mind news stories about entrepreneurs who set up shop to provide low-cost assistance in such legal matters as real estate transfers, uncontested divorces, and will preparation. While these renegade legal entrepreneurs have received a fair amount of attention recently, less publicized conflicts between lawyers and other professionals have existed for many years. From time to time, accountants, real estate agents, trust officers, insurance salespeople, financial planners, title insurance companies, and debt collection agencies have all been accused of engaging in the unauthorized practice of law. The issue is one of overlap between the legal profession and the well-established occupational practices of other professions.

These conflicts have generally resulted from changing business practices. In Abe Lincoln's day, people typically turned to lawyers to handle just about any financial matter that required special knowledge or that even remotely related to the law. Historically, it was the family lawyer who was the best educated person in the community and often the only person capable of handling such matters. The socioeconomic changes during the first part of this century, which included the development of our modern corporate system of business and an infinitely more complex tax structure, gave rise to a multitude of professionals from whom people could seek advice regarding financial concerns and other matters involving legal issues of one degree or another. The more recent emergence of sophisticated planned giving techniques, and the rapid increase in the number of development professionals employed by nonprofits, are trends which could conceivably lead to the unauthorized practice of law by unsuspecting development officers.

A brief review of the case law failed to uncover any unauthorized practice of law cases involving our colleagues in the development field, but did reveal a multitude of cases involving other non-lawyer professionals, including trust officers and financial planners. A quick examination of a few of these cases provides basic information on the topic and some important clues as to how development officers might avoid having their names printed in the law books.

Before accusing someone of engaging in the unauthorized practice of law, we need to have some idea of what the "practice of law" entails. As is the case with obscenity, the courts have been unable to define the "practice of law," but they know it when they see it.

The courts have established three categories of legal practice:

1. in court representation,
2. preparation of pleadings and legal documents,
3. the giving of "legal advice."

The first area is fairly easy to define and control. The second area becomes more difficult, as in the case of a real estate agent assisting in the preparation of documents leading to the sale of property. The third area is, of course, the most difficult of all to define, and it is here where development officers would be most likely to cross the line into the realm reserved for members of the bar. If so, it would be no defense that the advice given was correct and provided without charge.

One frequently cited Florida case *broadly* defined the practice of law as any advice or service which:

1. affects important legal rights,

2. requires more skill than possessed by the average person,

3. is performed for another.

A more recent case from the same state involving an insurance salesman who was setting up pension plans defines the practice of law as "the application of general rules of law to particular sets of facts as they relate to particular persons or legal entities." The court enjoined the insurance salesman from continuing to provide specific advice, but went on to hold that a discussion of general principles of law without applying those principles to particular factual situations does not constitute the practice of law and is thus acceptable behavior for non-lawyers.

This distinction between providing general legal information and applying the law to specific facts is found in other cases, such as an Ohio Supreme Court case which enjoined a bank trust department from ". . . offering or providing specific comments or advice on the form of investments or on the management of assets in a particular estate for the purpose of obtaining for a particular person or persons a more beneficial estate condition in relation to the tax and other consequences of death upon the estate."

There have also been "estate planning declarations" agreed to by state bar associations and banks which make it clear that trust officers (and presumably all other non-lawyers) can give general advice on common estate problems. Moreover, one such declaration noted that trust officers could make very specific recommendations when speaking *to the lawyer* responsible for preparing an estate plan. Likewise, bar associations have conferred with the accounting profession and guidelines have been established in an effort to clarify the role of accountants in matters relating to tax law.

The field of development is, of course, an area which continues to evolve and which is less well established than many other professions. What would the courts think of our computer software programs which can generate detailed planned giving proposals based on specific facts? What about the planned giving, financial planning, or estate planning seminars that are sometimes conducted by development officers? Just how "general" do we in the development field have to be in working with potential donors?

The few hours of legal research which went into writing this article left me with more questions than answers. There may well be no definitive answers to many of the questions we have in this area. One thing that is clear, however, is the underlying reason behind the effort to prohibit non-lawyers from engaging in any behavior defined as "practicing law." The reason, of course, is to protect the public from falling victim to incompetent advice on matters which affect important legal rights. Likewise, our concern about the unauthorized practice of law should be motivated by a desire to serve the best interest of our potential donors.

With the donor's interest in mind, we should be very sensitive to the need for competent legal counsel anytime specific issues of law are involved. We should be knowledgeable regarding the issue of unauthorized practice of law (perhaps by reviewing cases from the state or states where we work) and we should seek legal advice on the subject before doing anything we suspect might cross the line into this area. However, I would also suggest that our role as development officers should ideally involve more than dispensing general information and sending potential donors off to a lawyer. The following are a few thoughts on how we might go about helping our potential donors obtain the best possible legal advice.

If our goal as development officers is to assist people in being good stewards and not merely to raise funds for the benefit of our organizations, then it would seem that we have an obligation to be a knowledgeable resource for our donors. We have available to us many opportunities to promote and facilitate good stewardship that in no way intrude upon the legal profession. By effectively and appropriately providing information and direction for our donors, we will not only do a better job of promoting good stewardship, but we will also greatly increase the likelihood that our donors rightfully perceive us as helpful advisors, and not merely as advocates for our institutions.

We should be concerned about the possible perception that we are overreaching, but not so cautious and concerned that we forgo opportunities to better serve our donors and our institutions. Two possible contributions we could make would be to refer our donors to exceptionally well-qualified lawyers and then to work effectively with those lawyers to accomplish the donors' charitable intentions.

In regard to finding well-qualified lawyers, a couple of stories about two very different lawyers come to mind. Gerry Spence, the famous trial lawyer from Wyoming known for his flamboyant style, was once asked how he developed his skills as a litigator. His response is something everyone who hires a lawyer, or refers someone to a lawyer, should keep in mind. "Well," said Spence, "I just kept trying cases. I kept piling up the dead bodies until I finally learned how."

Young, inexperienced lawyers are not the only producers of "dead bodies." I think of a lawyer whose firm I clerked for while in law school. In his mid-forties, he had risen to the pinnacle of his profession. He was nationally recognized for his expertise in a particular field of law. The only thing more inflated than his hourly rate was his ego. It became apparent that part of the price he paid for "success" was a drug addiction. Although he eventually recovered, many of his former clients never will.

The lesson in these stories is simply to approach lawyers with a healthy degree of skepticism. Get to know them. Judge them by more than the size of their firms or the prestige of their alma maters.

Many of us may have some degree of familiarity with attorneys experienced in estate planning and tax law to whom we could, and perhaps already have, referred donors. I would suggest that we attempt to cultivate good relationships with these lawyers just as we cultivate donors. Let them know up front that you are interested in getting to know more about their method of operation. How do they work with clients? What kind of fees do they charge? Do they work well with their clients' other advisors, such as accountants and trust officers? How do they feel about involving a development officer in the process? How much time does it take them to perform various legal tasks? How much do they know about planned giving? What are their feelings about your institution? Do they return phone calls within a reasonable time? Ask the lawyer all these questions, but also ask former clients and non-lawyer professionals with whom the lawyer has worked.

One way to cultivate lawyers is to ask them to take part in a planned giving seminar at your institution. Many lawyers will appreciate opportunities to speak to a group of potential clients. Lawyers who specialize in estate planning may also be able to refer potential donors to you.

Finally, be cautious but not too shy about working with a lawyer to whom you have referred a donor. Hopefully, this is a subject the two of you will have discussed before a donor is referred. If possible, discuss specific planned giving strategies. Remember, the limitations as to how specific you can be in your discussions with donors do not apply to your discussions with their attorneys. Also, take the opportunity to ask specific questions pertinent to the gift or gifts coming to your institution—questions your donor might not be able to answer quite so readily. However, when communicating with a donor's attorney, never forget that the attorney's sole responsibility is to his or her client. Our challenge is to help lawyers understand that we can be of some assistance as they attempt to serve their clients.

Ideally, the involvement of a development officer as well as other non-lawyer advisors will make for a better client and a better lawyer. The client will be better informed as to what his or her goals are, and should be better able to communicate with the lawyer. The lawyer may be challenged to explore options not initially contemplated and may be able to complete the process in a shorter period of time as a result of the client's level of preparedness. In the end, the interest of the client/donor will be better served and the position of the institutions we serve will be enhanced.

A Checklist for
Development Committee Members

John W. Zehring

The Quakers have an interesting tradition which they call "queries." Friends use the form of a query to test themselves as to their own faithfulness. For example, one query is "Are we living and growing in the faith? Do we recognize growth when we see it and experience it?" Another is, "Are we eliminating those aspects of our life that place us in competition with one another rather than being supportive of one another?"

Such a tradition and device can serve well in many circumstances. A query you ask yourself is a high form of self-discipline, an internal taking of bearings to determine that you are on the right course.

As you reflect on your membership on a seminary development committee, consider some of the following queries to ask yourself:

Do I consider my board membership at the seminary among the top three or four activities in my life? Membership on the seminary's board should never be less than third place among your volunteer activities. Your church membership would be first place. Perhaps another school or a charity claims second place. To place your commitment to the seminary less than third place may weaken the contribution of time, wisdom, and resources that you can offer to this membership.

Have I actively solicited other board members on behalf of the seminary? This is the development committee's number one job: to encourage and promote heightened board support for the seminary. It should be the top priority for discussion at every development committee meeting. How can we move the board to new levels of leadership giving, both as a symbol to others and to support the operational needs of the school?

Have I made my own gift first? Development committee members need to set an example and a standard for giving. One of the commandments of fund raising is that no one can solicit another before he or she has made his or her own gift. Am I among the first to pledge my support? Do I pay promptly, without needing to be sent a reminder? Have I increased my gift annually?

Am I fully aware of all of the development programs? Do I understand fund raising's three-legged stool of annual gifts, planned gifts, and major or campaign gifts? Do I know about named funds, endowed scholarships, capital campaign plans? Do I comprehend the staff and resources the school has to fulfill its programs? Am I an advocate for a growing development program within the board of trustees?

Have I scouted for names of prospective donors which I passed on to the seminary? Members of the development committee should be the most important source of identifying new friends of the seminary. Have I regularly examined my network of contacts to suggest names, addresses, and background information of people who might be able to help the seminary? Have I set goals for myself for the number of people I will try to recommend each year? Have I introduced the president to prospective donors?

Have I offered to host a cultivation luncheon or dinner in my home? Development committee members shouldn't wait to be asked. Offer to invite contacts and prospective donors to your home for a meal to meet the seminary president and senior development officer. This is even more valuable to the seminary if you live at a distance, where the seminary may not have as high a presence as it does closer to campus.

Have I taken initiative to invite new people to seminary events? When there is a dinner, lecture, presentation, or special event, do I invite others to accompany me as a way of introducing them to the school?

Do I fully understand what the school itself identifies as its highest priority needs? If the annual fund for the operating budget is the highest priority, am I attuned to that priority?

Have I spoken a good word for the school wherever I can? Do I "talk it up" among my friends, associates, colleagues, clubs, and volunteer activities?

Have I been diligent in keeping the seminary's presence high among members of my church? Have I asked my church to support the seminary financially and by recommending prospective students? Do I make seminary materials readily available in my church? Have I helped bridge the gap between school and church?

Have I included the seminary in my will? Development committee members should do as they desire others to do. Have I tithed my estate? Have I informed the seminary that they are included in my will? Do I allow the seminary to use my act as an illustration in the solicitation of others?

Have I considered a planned gift with the seminary? Have I requested an estimate of benefits for a charitable gift annuity or pooled income fund? Have I invited a member of the development staff to explain how I might benefit from a planned gift? Planned gifts can sometimes be made for as little as $1,000 and, especially for seminaries just starting a planned gift program, serve as a needed base and inspiration for others.

Have I read materials sent in advance of meetings and prepared thoughtful comments and questions?

Have I read all of the school's current publications and promotional materials? Have I encouraged the highest standards for how the school's materials appear? Am I well acquainted with the catalog, brochures, newsletters, quarterly mailings, and other materials?

Have I taken the senior development officer to lunch? Get to know and develop a close working relationship with the senior staff member who services the committee.

Do I correspond with the seminary between development committee meetings? Do I send the development officer or president clippings, sample fund appeals from other institutions, ideas and suggestions?

Have I offered to underwrite special projects? Have I suggested ideas, like a new publication or event, where I have offered to underwrite the costs?

Have I participated in the life of the seminary beyond board and committee meetings? Have I attended classes, spoken with faculty and students, come to events, and supported important activities with my presence?

Am I able to state the case for the seminary clearly and briefly? Could I write the case for support on the back of a business card? Am I aware of the school's distinctive qualities and unique traits? Could I argue why a student should attend *this* school?

Am I well acquainted with the school's long-range plan? Do I know its plans, programs, needs, and dreams? Have I read and studied written plans for the future? Can I articulate the vision of the leadership to others?

Have I promoted the highest standards of excellence for the school? Do I insist that the school become the best that it can be? Am I a gadfly for raising vision and sights to higher levels? Do I feel responsible for the vision of the seminary?

Do I ask and ask and ask? The appropriate role of development committee members is not only to react but to initiate action. For the development committee, that action is primarily asking. It is important to invite, cultivate, promote, inform, nurture, identify, and evaluate. But most important, the job of development committee members is to ask.

To dwell on these queries constantly would be distracting. Yet, it is worthwhile for all members of a seminary development committee to review, occasionally, why and how well they do what they do.

Perhaps the idea of queries will stimulate your development committee to design its own checklist for reviewing its service: a device to help you focus and reflect on the task which is so central to your membership and ministry on the board.

Chapter Seven:
Balancing Personal
and Professional Lives

Suggestions on
Living a Measured Life

David P. Harkins

Over-extended, under-nourished, burned out, too much to do, and insufficient resources are but some of the liabilities extended to development professionals. How do we care for and nurture the assets and net worth of our personal and professional lives?

Each of us tries to do our job to the best of our ability and we work at that in a variety of ways. One way is to be alert to related literature. This can include *Seminary Development News, The Chronicle of Higher Education,* the *Wall Street Journal,* publications from professional organizations like the Association of Governing Boards, and resources from our bookstores. But we can do this in other ways, as well.

Seek involvement with colleagues and peers, particularly those who may be one step above you in their development. Develop networks among colleagues whom you can call for advice and help.

Participate in seminars, programs, and workshops. Don't go just for the sake of going. Analyze program content to make certain there is something of value.

Be willing to provide leadership as a workshop or discussion leader. It's no secret that the teacher often learns more than the student. Ask leaders of your professional group to help you identify opportunities to serve and provide leadership.

We need to attend to the spiritual dimension of our lives. We are exposed to the gratitude and depth of the spiritual gifts of many donors, but we are also drawn to the recognition that the gospel always calls us to do more, no matter how much we already do. Consider some suggestions:

Resist the danger of allowing the seminary (our employer) to be our substitute church. The real spiritual dimension of our lives may be strengthened within a congregational setting.

Work at understanding development as ministry, perhaps along with other professional colleagues.

Provide leadership in the church beyond fund raising issues. Do something different from what you do at work.

One of the best ways to avoid burnout is to strive to live a measured, balanced life. Balance often comes from self-discipline. Seek disciplines to protect your intellectual, social, and physical life. Also:

Vary your life at work, continuing to seek growth points.

Volunteer with organizations in the community, carefully choosing those which you find beneficial.

Be a consultant. If you have room and energy, make yourself available to others, either as a volunteer or in a paid capacity. Consulting extends the image of your employer. We grow and are energized by reaching beyond ourselves.

Plan time carefully and recognize priorities to those closest: a spouse, family, and others. When you are most over-extended at work, you are most in need of emphasis on some protected family time.

Offset travel with quality time. After an extended trip provide your spouse or your family with a night out together. Treat your family to the same style you enjoy on the road or when entertaining prospective donors. You provide a first-rate dinner for your most important constituents. Why not give your family the same?

Protect some evenings and some weekends. These should be as important as any item on your calendar.

Take a family member with you on a business trip. Do your business but set aside time for something special. If you have children take them individually on occasion for a "business lunch."

Take vacations, long and short. Time away will give you and your employer a greater appreciation for your work and render you more effective. Treat yourself to vacations on the same level as those you take on the expense account.

Manage time for your professional life, your spiritual life, your family life—and time for yourself. What does it benefit your seminary if you exceed the goals for a year or two and then burn out?

Nine Rules to Live By

David Heetland

Someone once remarked that there are three irrefutable rules in fund raising. This person went on to say that unfortunately no one has ever discovered what they are. Preparing for this presentation caused me to reflect on the rules which guide me in my development work. They are not irrefutable, and I couldn't limit them to three. I would like to share with you, however, nine rules I try to live by. I am *not* suggesting these should be your rules, but in hearing mine perhaps you will be encouraged to reflect upon and clarify those unwritten rules which guide you in your work.

1. Remember that development work is ministry. I got into development basically because I was coerced. I've stayed in development because I've come to recognize that development is one of the most important ministries that can be performed. We have the privilege to model what it means to be good stewards—of finances, of time, of life itself—and to invite others to grow in their stewardship. The greatest satisfactions for me in this work come when I feel I have helped others experience life more fully by investing themselves in something beyond themselves.

2. Develop goals. I like development because I am a goal-oriented person, and I happen to believe that little is achieved without goals. I set yearly, monthly, and daily goals for myself. In addition to dollar goals, I set goals for the number of visits I hope to make each month, the number of leadership donors I hope to have at the end of the year, and so on. Each month as I set new goals for the month ahead, I also evaluate my progress on the previous month's goals. Having goals helps keep me focused on what is important.

3. Practice time management. I believe that time management is essential to reach my goals. We all know various time management techniques. The three that have been most helpful to me are saying no to all projects and activities that do little or nothing to advance my long-term goals; avoiding all meetings that do nothing to advance my goals; and using a Day-Timer, one book that serves as my calendar, daily task list, appointment book, expense record, journal, address book, and tickler file. I call this book my "second Bible," and it goes nearly everywhere with me.

4. *Stay externally focused.* I push myself, and my staff, to be out of the office as much as in. Months in advance I will schedule blocks of time to be out—even though I have no idea where I'll be. That becomes "sacred time" and I keep it clear of meetings and all internal activities which otherwise tend to consume my calendar and trivialize my development goals. I believe there is no magic in development. It simply requires visibility, perseverance, hard work, and staying externally focused.

5. *Continue growing in development.* Growth, for me, takes place through reading, writing, and attending seminars. My goals include attending at least one seminar a year and setting aside some days each year for reading and writing. One of the special values of DIAP seminars is building relationships with other development professionals in theological education. I consider my DIAP colleagues my best mentors, and I love picking their brains about what has and has not worked for them.

6. *Maintain peak health.* The best way I've discovered to handle the rigors of development work is to maintain peak health through proper exercise and nutrition. I'm a bit of an exercise and health nut, and I try to exercise daily and eat a low-fat, vegetarian diet. This program serves me well and is also a great stress reducer. The challenge, of course, is to maintain such a program "on the road." It can be done, but it requires a good deal of creativity.

7. *Seek balance in daily life.* Bradford Murphy, a psychiatrist, said a healthy life is like a table with four legs—work, play, love, and worship—and he added that he would place a bouquet of flowers on the table to celebrate each day. I treasure that anal-

ogy and use it as a reminder that life's beauty and preciousness are to be savored daily, and the way to do so is by building play, love, and worship—as well as work—into each day.

8. Recognize the need for rest. One of my most important discoveries was that development work is never done. Therefore I could either work twenty-four hours a day, or I could recognize my need for rest. I'm a slow learner, but I now recognize the importance of rest—time when mind and body can be freed from busyness and rejuvenated. I take seriously the need for a good night's sleep, some time off each week, and regular vacation time. I am convinced that this time of rest can be a time of re-creation that brings healing, wholeness, and new creativity into my life.

9. Laugh at life, and especially at yourself. I try not to take life, or myself, too seriously. My development colleagues still laugh at an incident that happened to me several years ago. I visited an elderly woman who was very deaf, but who refused to invite me to her apartment. Instead we sat in the main lobby next to the switchboard operator. In the midst of this noisy, very public setting I tried to discreetly ask her about her estate plans. I don't think she heard half of what I said. Finally she agreed to walk next door to a restaurant where there would be a bit more privacy. As we got up to leave, she turned to the switchboard operator, and in a stage whisper loud enough for the whole world to hear, said, "I can't get rid of him. He is so *boring!*"

I will conclude on that note, before you say the same thing!

Religious Leadership: Our Vocation

Alicia Forsey

When I was studying as an undergraduate philosophy major, I had the good fortune of having theologian Jacob Needleman as a professor. He taught me that religion can be an important influence in addressing the problems of our culture, and that at the heart of all great religions we will find the same truths. I also took a philosophy course which looked at Prescriptivism. Prescriptivists make every effort to live in accordance with what they say they believe. I thought it made perfect sense. I talked about not being cruel to animals. Prescriptivism put me in the position of knowing I was a hypocrite if I said I was against cruelty to animals and then ate them, so I became a vegetarian. If I said I was concerned about the environment and about pollution, and yet I still drove a car for convenience sake, then I was a hypocrite. I gave my car away.

Then one day, about a year later, I was standing at a bus stop in the rain—a baby under one arm and a bag of groceries under the other. I felt very discouraged. I noticed that there was more traffic on the street than I remembered ever seeing. Obviously, my own dedication to living by what I said I believed had not translated into anything changing beyond my personal life. Here the light bulb went on: *Leadership!* I had changed my personal life—a good start—but I had done nothing to take my concerns beyond myself. I needed to study religious leadership.

I attended seminary, graduated, and was ordained. But somehow I wound up in what I think of as the "real world," and not in the church. This is probably a good thing as coffee hour after Sunday service is my version of hell. I felt that the work I was doing was a form of religious leadership. I was working for children at risk in places like East Oakland. I was moving resources from where they were abundant to where (in my opinion) they were most needed—for elementary school, inner-city children. This real world was no picnic. It meant working for children who lived in neighborhoods that were not safe places, where there was little hope for the future.

After twelve years of working in this environment I was thrilled when the president of my seminary asked me to return to complete a capital campaign. I felt as if I was ready for a "kinder, gentler place." I thought raising money for my old alma mater would be a piece of cake.

Returning as staff to the seminary I had known and loved as a student was one of the most painful experiences in my professional career. The seminary's development efforts were looked upon with much ambivalence. I knew that faculty avoided me because I was in the position of being one who undertakes a "necessary evil." The task of raising funds to support our religious institutions was necessary, but certainly a distraction from the loftier, theological realms where the life-force of the institution held court.

I could have quit my job at the seminary and returned to the real world where my efforts were always appreciated, but I decided that I would stick it out and try to make a difference. Education makes change possible. I realized that I had to learn how to articulate fund raising in such a way that it would be understood and accepted as a vital part of the whole institution. I had to find a way to ground fund raising in the realm of theology. I am grateful to Helen Luke for giving me the key which unlocked the first doors toward changing the way my board, faculty, and staff think about money.

Luke, in her book *Woman Earth and Spirit,* reminds us that money was originally intended to be a symbol of exchange. Money came out of the barter system where what was received was equal to what was given. The coin, with a symbol of the sacred on one side and a symbol of the secular on the other, was equal in value to the loaf of bread, or whatever was being exchanged. The focus was on the *exchange,* not on the symbol that made it possible.

Our work is all about relationships. We are not "arm-twisters" or "hit-men." We are engaged in the business of establishing right relationships. If we look at our work in this way—as a way of establishing a fair exchange—we have placed one foot in the realm of the theoretical and the other in the realm of the practical, making ourselves a bridge across the chasm that has caused so many difficulties in our religious institutions.

Imagine what our world would look like if we thought of all of our ways of engaging in exchange (words, touch, gestures, tangible symbols that pass between us, such as money) as ways we use our own resources. If words were not looked upon as being disposable, we would be committed to keeping our conversations grounded in our being. We would think in terms of dialogue, balanced conversation that reflected a fair exchange between us. We would leave coffee hour replenished, not depleted.

Religious leadership is part of our vocation. We all must educate our boards, faculty, and staff about the true meaning of stewardship. If we hope to integrate the work of the development office into the life of our seminaries, it is up to us to find a way to do so.

I am looking for ways to address the leadership issues of our seminaries. I am studying diverse styles—from Robert Greenleaf, who teaches a collaborative style, to James Fisher, who believes that collaborative leadership is an oxymoron. I am especially encouraged by the work of DIAP and by publications such as *The Reluctant Steward,* which indicate that the gap between the theoretical and the practical is a crucial issue facing our seminaries. We are the missing link in this gap, and we have to look for ways to build an integrated approach to gathering resources for our seminaries.

I'm glad I didn't leave my seminary. Our president, now beginning her fourth year, is a person of uncommon vision. Trustees have a better sense of what development work is all about. I feel more integrated into the life of my school. I know that I will need to continue talking about stewardship in the truest sense of the word—in terms of relationship and exchange—as new board members, students, faculty, and staff come to the seminary. I know that I have to never let stewardship become a buzzword for fund raising.

Maya Angelou described stewardship in simple, straightforward terms at a conference I attended. She stood before hundreds of people and said, "I know that I did not pay the price for me to be here. Someone else paid that price." She went on to say that in her work she is always aware of her responsibility for paving the way for people who follow after her, for continuing the dedication, the commitment, the stewardship of people who came before her. She is in the middle. In our positions as seminary development officers, we are all in the middle.

Development as a Calling

Anita Rook

In contemplating this article I was reminded of an old *Shoe* cartoon in which Skyler asks Uncle Cosmo, "What's a career?" and Uncle Cosmo responds, "That's a job that's dragged on much too long."

While some days the frustrations and disappointments of development work may leave me with the feeling that my career is a job that's lasted too long, it is more often rewarding and fulfilling. For me, development has been a calling. While I was only vaguely aware of the call at the beginning, I came away from the interview for my first position at Loyola Marymount University with a sense that there was important work going on in the development department and that I would find it meaningful to be a part of the team. Within less than a year the call became less vague, and at the end of three years I knew that helping organizations and donors achieve mutually satisfying goals, intended to make our world a better place, was my vocation. I have tried to organize some thoughts around two broad themes that have been important aspects of my career—professional and personal growth and relationships.

Paraphrasing Robert Fulghum, I think that everything I needed to know about the techniques of fund raising I learned in my first three years in the "kindergarten" of Loyola Marymount. The learning came by "doing" under the mentoring and coaching of four individuals: a Catholic sister, a development professional who had cut his fund raising teeth in the March of Dimes and then higher education, and two volunteers who were also major donors. It became clear quite early that the techniques of fund raising are relatively easy to grasp and practice. What is difficult is the artful application of these techniques in diverse settings and with diverse constituencies. This is what development is all about, and the art must always be learned and relearned. No sooner do I think I have learned the art than a situation will arise in which the artful application has to be created again.

Throughout the years I have been blessed with many more mentors who have guided me in the art of development. I also have had the privilege of being a mentor to women and men. These opportunities to help someone else have invariably been as helpful to me because of what I learned during the relationship.

Until recent years, our sector did not have a very large body of literature, and I found it necessary to find other resources from which to continue to learn. The literature and educational offerings in leadership development, management, organization development, psychology, marketing, and adult learning theories, addressed primarily to the for-profit sector, were where I found fresh ideas and concepts which could be translated and reinterpreted for nonprofit management and development.

I still try to increase my professional capacities by reading Max De Pree, Warren Bennis, Peter Drucker, Stephen Covey, James Autrey, and a host of others plus the many new materials prepared specifically for the nonprofit sector. However, in recent years personal and spiritual development have begun to take precedence over professional development. A Christian classics Sunday school class in my congregation has helped give direction to my reading. C.S. Lewis' *Mere Christianity,* Lewis Smedes' *Mere Morality, The Westminster Confession of Faith,* and Bonhoeffer's *The Cost of Discipleship* are among the books that have given me the opportunity to explore other dimensions of growth that are integral to both my personal and professional self.

A friend recently introduced me to a book which, while not explicitly spiritual in nature, has great potential for stimulating my personal growth—*Pigs Eat Wolves: Going Into Partnership With Our Dark Side.* Charles Bates uses the full version of the three little pigs fable to help us understand that there is probably a wolf and each of the three little pigs in all of us. He contends that most of us are stuck at second pig thinking and keep using solutions that didn't work before to try to solve new problems. He points us in the direction of developing third pig thinking—understanding the way the wolf thinks and moving beyond. I know I have been stuck at second pig thinking and want to see if I can learn to do third pig thinking.

Fundamentally, development is about creating and growing relationships with people around shared hopes, visions, and desires to make a positive difference. In looking back, I can identify that the times I have been successful and the times I have failed were inextricably linked to my faithfulness in keeping relationships in the right order, understanding the complexities of the relationships, and being more concerned about others than about myself. My first responsibility is my relationship with God, and if that is right then relationships with family, professional colleagues, and friends can be right. When I fail to pay attention to my relationship with God, I will fail in other relationships.

Within a week of leaving this conference two years ago, my president informed me that he no longer wanted me in the position of vice president for development. His decision was not based on my technical competency for the position. It was a failure of relationships. Although this was a painful experience it has pushed me to grow and learn more about myself. I have been able to reconfirm that in my career I have most often filled the role of construction manager, teacher, and coach.

At the time I was asked to leave, Mary Catherine Bateson's *Composing a Life* came to my attention. It tells the stories of five women, including the author, and how they have gone about composing their lives in the midst of change, broken relationships, and in positive and negative environments. This book and many other resources, including the counsel of friends and colleagues, have helped me reunderstand that our lives are in a constant state of composition. We are all works in progress and part of our ongoing challenge is to recognize that there is always a purpose to the places we have been and the places we will go. The purpose may not always be the one we defined but was or is the one that God defines.

So, in some ways I am back where I started with the

question, "Is this a career or just a job that's lasted too long?" I have to say that I don't know yet. I am still seeking guidance for that answer, and there are two verses which I often turn to when the answers don't seem to be clear: Hebrews 11:1 and 12:1— "faith is being sure of what we hope for and certain of what we do not see. . . . since we are surrounded by such a great cloud of witnesses, let us throw off everything that hinders and the sin that so easily entangles, and let us run with perseverance the race that God sets before us."

My Life in Development

David P. Harkins

I may be one of a few persons in this setting who made an intentional decision to become a development officer. Most of us have found our way into this work because we have been challenged to do it, we have been told that we have particular skills that are needed. In my case, I was a college business manager, and I found myself being very critical of the development function at the institution where I worked.

That critical reaction was not articulated or used in a confrontive way within the institution. However, as a member of the senior administrative staff I felt the development function just wasn't being done the way it ought to be, that the institution was not gaining maximum advantage for its investment, and that its constituencies were not being appropriately challenged.

Finally I said to myself, "If you really think you have some ideas about this, why don't you find a way to try them out?" Some friends knew of my interest in looking at development possibilities. It was that interest, together with a commitment to church-related higher education and a love for the church, that ultimately caused me to move to the vice presidency of a seminary.

My mentor in this effort has been our mutual colleague, Fred Hofheinz of the Lilly Endowment. We essentially cut our eye teeth together. Upon arriving at the seminary I was brash enough to write a letter to Bob Lynn, who had just been named vice president for the religion division of the Lilly Endowment. I wrote him, saying "Here are some of the needs of this institution." I gave him a shopping list. He wrote back, recognizing I was in need of help, and said, "You really need to talk with my new colleague, Fred Hofheinz." We got together, and through that relationship I have seen much happen in the development enterprise in theological education.

I thought I had assessed the picture pretty well when I came to the seminary, but I had missed on two counts. I did not know that the business manager believed that every dime the institution spent on development was wasted money. He believed that every gift that came, regardless of its source, regardless of the involvement in generating it, would have come anyway. I also was not alert to the fact that the president believed that he had not been called to the seminary to raise money. It became clear that he had hired me to do this task, and that his role in fund raising would be minimal.

There also seemed to emanate from the seminary's professional advisors, specifically the auditors and investment managers, an understanding that their role was to monitor the demise of the institution. In their judgment it was not likely that the institution would survive a change of administrative leadership.

These, obviously, were not my ideas as to why I had been brought into this position, nor did they reflect my interest in getting a strong development program in place. Twenty years later the institution survives—and with some degree of financial health.

I've been asked what I think are my most significant accomplishments. While there are all kinds of reasons for us to do what we do, I think the primary reasons are personal fulfillment and the sustaining of whatever we define as quality of life for our families. My wife, Sharon, and I share great pride in our family. I am aware that they are who they are because of what she has given them while I have been off doing my part for the family by getting my job done, so the primary accomplishment is hers.

Other sources of pride include the fact that the institution which I continue to serve is alive and has at least a degree of financial health, and the strength of the DIAP organization.

For those of you who don't know, DIAP grew out of a series of programs and the strong interest of the Lilly Endowment to seek ways to strengthen the development function in theological education—believing this was the way to strengthen the whole enterprise. In the mid-seventies Lilly sponsored a series of competitive grants programs in which they invited seminaries to submit proposals on a variety of issues. In one of those programs there were five offerings. I initiated five proposals, and I am told it is the only time Fred Hofheinz can remember issuing five rejection letters to an institution almost simultaneously. It was out of that experience that I called Fred Hofheinz and said, "Obviously I need help"—and so we spent time together.

Later I was asked to be part of a review panel for another set of competitive grants in which I did not submit proposals. We finished our assigned tasks, making recommendations to the endowment staff that several grants be awarded. Those of us on the reading panel also asked for a dialogue with Fred Hofheinz and Charles Johnson. We told them that our greater concern was for those who were the losers. It was clear that considerable help was needed to strengthen the development function in theological education. Lilly responded, offering an opportunity for several institutions to invite people to serve as new development officers in theological education. They provided salary supplements and a teaching/learning environment with faculty members serving as mentors to new colleagues.

The next step looked at the total enterprise. Thus, the DIAP program was established. The original proposal called for an advisory committee to work in a modest way with consultants who would really do the work. I can overstate the case by saying that at the first meeting of the advisory committee we fired the consultants! Actually, we allowed them to work with us through the first year. However, it was not a good relationship and it was clear we had to seek our own way. We were the insiders who could identify the needs and find ways to address them.

What are the disappointments? For me, the realization that at my seminary we still have not developed a strong cadre of major gift prospects. That does not bode well for the sustained strength of the seminary. I am also disturbed that in spite of all our collective work the church is quite fractionalized. This means the church is unable to be about its task of improving the quality of life for others. I think the church is the last remaining vestige that can accomplish this task. Somehow it must come to its own wholeness and address the critical needs of our society rather than struggle with its own bureaucracy.

Our staff juggles priorities, leaving much on the table to be done. In the midst of this we say to one another that it is important to set aside time and space to be away, and to develop networks with professional colleagues. For such times I am grateful.

Study Leaves
for Development Officers

David Heetland

For the last three months I have escaped airports, hotel rooms, and committee meetings. How have I done it? By taking a three-month paid study leave. What was the purpose? Reflection, study, and self-renewal. Today is the last day of that leave. As I look back on this time away from the regular demands of development work, I realize how valuable it has been.

Recently our seminary developed a study leave policy for senior administrators who have been with the institution for some time. I was privileged to be the first one to take a leave. I am convinced that such leaves offer several benefits to both the individual and the institution, and I would encourage my colleagues at other institutions to explore the study leave possibility.

Benefits to Development Officers

Time for reflection. Development work is so action oriented that we seldom take the necessary time to pause and reflect on what we are doing and where we are going. The study leave gave me ample opportunity to reflect on long-range goals and priorities, both personal and professional, and to set new goals for myself.

Opportunity for serious study. Most of us are affiliated with academic communities because we are invigorated by the intellectual climate. Yet, there is little time for us to take advantage of it or to contribute to it. The study leave provided me with the time to read widely in my own field, to read some of the works of my faculty colleagues, and to prepare a book manuscript and a course which I hope to teach next year.

Time for self-renewal. Faculty members frequently seek

renewal through travel. However, since I am on the road so much of the time I sought renewal by staying home! The renewal of energy and enthusiasm came in a variety of ways: learning how to use the computer, pursuing avocational interests, exploring parts of my own community, doing volunteer work, and spending precious time with my family.

Benefits to Institutions

Encouraging longevity and stability of an administrative team. An administrative team that works well together is a valuable asset to any institution, and ways need to be found to recognize and reward such teamwork. The study leave is an attractive option, especially when pay raises cannot always match competitive offers from other institutions. With a shortage of qualified development professionals and with salaries soaring, institutions wishing to keep their development staff in place might well benefit from a study leave policy.

Enhancing the skills, strengths, and insights of those on leave. I trust that my newly developed computer skills will enhance not only my personal life, but also my professional life. The course I hope to teach will satisfy a personal goal, but will also enhance the seminary's offerings. My readings have given me some new ideas that I look forward to trying out. In these several ways I believe the study leave has enhanced my professionalism and made me an even more valuable member of the administrative team.

Self-renewal benefits the institution as well as the individual. I feel a renewed sense of dedication to my work. I am ready to travel again, and I am enthusiastic and excited about my profession. The seminary receives the benefit of stability and renewed enthusiasm—not a bad combination.

Designing a Study Leave

If you would like to consider the possibility of a study leave, I would offer the following recommendations:

Explore the possibility as a part of your annual evalua-

tion. Have you been at the institution for at least five years? Has there been growth in the seminary's development program during this time? Are you a valued member of the administrative team? If you can answer yes to these questions you are a likely candidate for a study leave.

Have some definite goals in mind which you hope to accomplish during your study leave. While renewal can take many forms, an institution will respond more favorably to a leave which is well thought out and is more substantive than a long vacation. My three major goals were to learn the computer, write a manuscript, and prepare to teach a course. The seminary supported these as valid goals, and I felt a sense of real accomplishment when each was completed.

Outline how the study leave will benefit the institution. Can you point to new skills that will be acquired which will enhance your job performance? Are there unmet institutional needs which you would like to address in a study leave? Is there something you can offer the institution as a result of the leave, such as a course, a new development program, or an article which strengthens the profession?

Prepare a plan describing how the development work will continue in your absence. Who will supervise the development effort? How will your responsibilities be handled? I am fortunate to have an able assistant who handled much of my daily work, and a dedicated staff who assumed additional responsibilities. I also spent a half day in the office each week meeting with staff and taking care of matters that needed my attention. As a result, the development program continued in full swing, the staff grew in their confidence to handle various responsibilities, and my study leave went very smoothly.

Work with the president to find a mutually convenient time to begin a study leave. In my case the study leave was a welcome goal at the end of a demanding capital campaign. Obviously it would not have been a good idea to take the leave in the midst of the campaign, nor when the campaign concluded. The calendar year, the development program, and the broader institutional goals were all taken into consideration.

Finally, work with the administrative team to develop a study leave policy for all senior administrators. There will be strong support for such a program if it is available to others beyond development. The administrative team, and ultimately the institution, will be further strengthened through this collaborative effort toward personal and professional growth.

Chapter Eight:
Looking Toward the Future

Institutional Planning:
the Foundation for Development

Daniel Conway

I was a freshman in our college seminary when Saint Meinrad started its development program. That was 1968, and like most development officers, I would not have believed it if someone had predicted then that twenty years later I would make development my career.

Although my involvement was minimal (I worked in the development office as a student), I remember that the early years were tough ones. The seminary was in a severe financial crisis, and there was enormous pressure on the development office to produce immediate results.

Fortunately, Saint Meinrad's first chief development officer, John MacCauley, was a true professional. He did not believe that a successful development program could be built overnight, and he insisted that we take the time to do it right.

In his view, "doing it right" meant institutional planning. It meant commitment to the future—by establishing priorities and by creating a strong climate of support for the seminary and its mission. And it meant a staunch refusal to allow negative thinking or crisis management to become part of our leadership style.

As a result of John MacCauley's vision, Saint Meinrad developed a leadership style that makes planning an integral part of development, which is defined as "a program of systematic growth." In fact, the three-fold purpose of Saint Meinrad's development program is to facilitate institutional planning, to communicate values, and to invite alums and friends to invest in seminary education at Saint Meinrad.

According to this view, one of the primary purposes of Saint Meinrad's development program is to serve as a catalyst for creating a strong sense of identity and mission among members of the Saint Meinrad community. This is the internal function of development. Through a process of critical self-examination and of strategic, long-range planning, members of the seminary community come to a deeper understanding of *who* they are (their mission and values) and of *what* they want to do (their long-term objectives and specific action plans).

This annual planning process gives development its most valuable and indispensable tool: the case for investment in the seminary's future. This "case statement," which is much more than an attractive brochure, communicates the seminary's purpose, its programs and activities, and its priority needs. This is the external function of development: to communicate with the seminary's various constituents and to invite their participation and support.

At Saint Meinrad, planning serves a double function: It builds confidence among internal and external constituents, and it sets the agenda for public relations and fund raising. As a result of planning, our communications materials (newsletters, brochures, audio-visual productions, et cetera) have a clearer focus. And our fund raising is not an end in itself. It is directly related to priorities which have been identified through long-range planning.

Of course, there are many kinds of planning, and over the years, Saint Meinrad has used a variety of planning methods. Five years ago, with the assistance of an alum, Joseph V. Quigley, president of Quigley & Associates, a management consulting firm based in Houston, Texas, we adopted the process known in business and in higher education as strategic planning.

From the development point of view, there are several advantages to the planning method recommended by Quigley & Associates. First, strategic planning pays particular attention to environmental factors, to what's going on outside of the seminary and by listening to the concerns of its various publics.

Second, the management conference approach to strategic planning emphasizes a leadership style that is both collaborative and decisive. It insists that the CEO play a central role in the formulation of the seminary's mission, values, and objectives. It also provides methods of collaboration and consultation that ensure a broad sense of ownership for the seminary's mission and for its future plans.

Finally, the strategic planning method we use at Saint Meinrad makes it possible for us to be held accountable for the success or failure of individual elements in the plan. This is an important reality factor. Too often planning resembles daydreaming or wishful thinking. Our plans sound good, but they aren't practical. By clearly identifying who, what, when, where, why, and how, planning becomes more practical and, therefore, more helpful as a management tool.

In our experience, good planning leads to good communications and good fund raising. Why? Because an institution which has a strong sense of identity and purpose is in a better position to reach out to alums and friends and invite them to invest in its future.

Our twenty years of experience in development has shown that, for us, planning, communications, and fund raising can never be separated. They are indispensable elements in the long-term growth of the institution and, therefore, they are necessary, complementary functions in our comprehensive development program.

Will it produce immediate results? Perhaps not. But to our way of thinking, planning is a way of life—not a "quick fix." And our experience over the last twenty years has convinced us that the long-term results are easily worth the investment.

Involving Friends
in Strategic Planning

David Heetland

Leaders of many educational institutions recognize the importance of strategic planning to provide a vision for the future that is compatible with their mission. Most, if not all, of these leaders also recognize that strategic planning should be a group effort. But who should be included in the planning group? Most institutions would probably include trustees, administrators, and faculty. Some would add alums and students.

At Garrett-Evangelical Theological Seminary we included all of the above constituencies in a year-long planning process designed to address the key issues facing the seminary. We also made the decision to include friends in this effort. Friends were defined as non-alums who had a demonstrated or a potential interest in the seminary. Volunteers and donors were considered, as well as persons who had special expertise or interest in theological education.

While some leaders were at first hesitant to add another constituency to the planning process, it proved to be so beneficial that we think it merits careful consideration by other institutions.

Benefits of Involving Friends

What were the benefits of involving friends in strategic planning?

1. They brought a perspective of persons not closely related to the institution. Their questions and insights were penetrating and proved to be extremely valuable. One administrator at first wondered aloud what persons with no affiliation to our institution could possibly contribute to a task force on faculty development. He later confided that he was pleasantly surprised to discover how much they had to offer.

2. Friends, faculty, and trustees also gained new respect

and appreciation for one another as they worked closely together on a common concern. One friend summed up the feelings of many when he said he had grown to deeply appreciate our faculty as a result of the strategic planning process.

3. Involving friends was a great way to expand awareness of our institution. Several friends who served on task forces had never been on campus before. Others knew us only superficially. Over the course of the year their awareness of our institution, and the challenges facing us, grew significantly.

4. Along with a heightened awareness came a greater commitment to the institution. Some who were not previously donors became donors. Others who were donors increased their giving. Several expressed interest in continuing their involvement with our institution.

5. Involving friends proved to be an excellent way to expand our volunteer base beyond our board of trustees and alum board. Another cadre of people now exists to help interpret and implement the strategic plan.

6. Involving friends in strategic planning also provided an excellent opportunity to test leadership potential. Several who served on strategic planning task forces have been invited to join the board of trustees, and one has become the new board chair.

Guidelines in Involving Friends

If you are interested in involving friends in your strategic planning process, you may want to consider the following guidelines:

1. Determine an appropriate balance among trustees, faculty, alums, administrators, students, and friends. Our strategic planning process included four task forces. Each task force was chaired by a trustee and consisted of 20 additional people: three trustees, three faculty, three alums, three administrators, three students, and five friends. This balance worked well in our situation. The key is to make sure that a group of people somewhat removed from an institution does not dominate the process, but is an important presence in the process.

2. After determining the appropriate number of friends to involve, invite suggestions of names from trustees and alums. These can be persons already affiliated with your institution, or they may have no previous affiliation. Persons should be nominated who demonstrate the same leadership qualities desired in trustees. The final list of suggestions should be considerably longer than needed as a number of people, perhaps as many as half, will be unable or unwilling to serve. The list should then be prioritized.

3. Starting at the top of the prioritized list these friends should be visited, preferably by a trustee and an administrator. The importance of the institution's strategic planning process should be discussed, along with some of the key issues facing the institution. Persons should be informed that they have been nominated to be a part of this process and their interest should be assessed.

4. If the strategic planning process involves a number of task forces, these should be explained. Friends should be encouraged if possible to express which area would have the greatest interest to them, and where they feel they could make the most meaningful contribution.

5. If persons express an interest and willingness to serve, follow up with a formal letter of invitation from the president and/or board chair. Accompanying the invitation should be a job description which clearly spells out the task force assignment and other expectations, such as the time line, number of meetings, and any other important details.

6. Once persons have accepted the invitation to serve, they should be provided with as much information as necessary to help them become productive members of the strategic planning process. Especially helpful is background information on the institution, materials related to their particular area of concern, and questions they will be expected to address.

If you decide to involve friends in your strategic planning process you may well find, as we did, that it is an energizing and positive addition to a most important process.

Can Today's Donors Be Replaced?

James M. Wray, Jr.

The usual $125 annual fund gift from a retired alum arrived last week. With the gift was a note saying, "Use wherever needed." In the same bundle of mail was a gift and letter from a young trustee. The letter directed the gift to an endowment fund in honor of his minister.

Common incidents? Perhaps they illustrate a change taking place among our donors—change urging us to give attention to how we will replace today's donors and who tomorrow's donors will be.

Who is the donor we are replacing? The typical seminary donor is a church person age fifty or older. These people have a strong commitment to the denomination with which they are affiliated. They are the products of a socialization process which instilled institutional loyalty and respect for authority. Their giving often demonstrates an unquestioning confidence in the institution and the chief executive officer. The phrase, "use wherever needed," reflects the values, commitments, and loyalties of a "graying generation."

On the other hand, the gift directed to a specific fund named in honor of the donor's minister demonstrates the motivation of the baby boomer generation. One only need recall the "turbulent sixties" to grasp the differences between these two generations. These differences will have significant impact on donor research, prospect cultivation, recruitment of volunteers, and solicitation of gifts as we replace today's donors with baby boomer donors.

We need to be mindful of the baby boomer generation and how this population will increasingly affect not only development programs, but institutions as well. At the same time, we would do well to intensify our efforts with the older generation.

Statistics suggest strong reason for doing so. Americans age fifty and older hold three-fourths of the accumulated wealth. We have about a ten-year window of opportunity with a generation that clearly has the wealth as well as a value system which places importance on the role of church and seminary in society.

Another characteristic of the older generation, in contrast to the younger generation, is its propensity for delayed gratification. A deferred gift "feels right" to one in this generation. Planning today for a future benefit is fulfilling.

The concentration of wealth, denominational and institutional loyalty, and inclination toward delayed gratification commend the older generation as one resource for replacing today's donors. However, we have a relatively short time period in which to bring more persons of this generation into a supportive relationship with our institutions. In time, institutions will depend solely on the baby boomers to support their mission. We must begin preparing now for that to happen. But first, who is this coming generation of donors?

Only five percent of this generation can be classified as "yuppies," making $40,000 or more annually. More than seventy percent of them earn an average of $10,000 a year. Disparity in the income and wealth of this generation will widen. For example, the total worth of estates in the U.S. is expected to rise from $924.1 billion between 1987-1991 to $2.1 trillion between 2007-2011. Baby boomers will be the principal inheritors of these estates. The average inheritance for ninety percent of them will be $40,000. Approximately $1.4 trillion will be concentrated in the hands of only ten percent of the baby boomers.

Denominational loyalty and identity are not important to this generation. Lyle Schaller has noted that a growing proportion of Protestant congregations, and a majority of the congregations averaging more than 3,000 in worship, do not have denominational affiliation. The baby boomers joining this growing segment of American Protestantism value biblical teaching and faith interpretation that help them deal with life.

Activism has been a trademark of this generation. That

trait is continuing through this generation's volunteerism. They expect a greater voice in determining policies. They are demanding about information and accountability.

A trend in the charitable giving of this generation is already discernible. Giving is more specific and connects the donor and institution. The baby boomer is more likely to make a short-term financial commitment than a long-term one. Some congregations are already conducting fund drives every six weeks. Others are experimenting with tithing commitments on a three-month basis.

These characteristics pose some concerns for our institutions:

What will be the role of planned giving in a generation that values instant gratification?

How will the annual fund be presented to a generation that requires specific, relational reasons for giving?

How will seminaries with a heritage of strong denominational identity and loyalty relate to a generation for whom such loyalty and identity are less important?

Can the church attract this generation to membership and thereby create a pool of potential donors for seminaries?

Will the activism of this generation redefine the role of trustees and other volunteers in our institutions?

We have a lot to learn about this generation. Having become more market and consumer oriented, the development enterprise is positioned well to bring this generation into supportive relationships. The baby boomer generation brings a new dimension to our institutional life. Will they support seminaries, and if so, what will be the extent of their influence once they wield financial power? Something dynamic is beginning to happen. Development officers need more information about the characteristics, motivations, and values of this younger generation in order to play an active role in bringing this population into the life of our seminaries.

Marketing Theological Education

William R. Cunitz

If you think some people in church-related institutions have difficulty with fund raising, wait until you hear them on the subject of marketing!

Members of Andover Newton's development staff expected some resistance from the seminary community to our proposal for a comprehensive market research study, but fully anticipated that the benefits would outweigh any potential for controversy. With regard to the critical issues of student recruitment, program delivery, and a compelling case for charitable support, we were convinced that market research, combined with strategic planning, held the key to the school's success for the 1990s.

My first exposure to the possibilities and application of market research for theological education was the result of an ATS development seminar several years ago. I lost my notes to the seminar, but did manage to pick up one of the recommended books, *Positioning,* by Al Ries and Jack Trout. It dramatically changed the way I viewed the application of marketing principles to the nonprofit world. In doing so, it provided an exciting option for our school's future.

As Andover Newton entered the 1990s, nagging deficit problems forced us to consider a number of budget balancing alternatives which ranged from drastic down-sizing to a planned short-term increase of the deficit by investing borrowed dollars in the future of the institution. Following a professional audit of the development department that acknowledged the need for additional staff and resources, the board of trustees voted to adopt a revenue enhancement plan that augmented the development staff by three, enlarged the deficit temporarily, and made provision for a year-long market research project.

Completed in July 1992, the first phase of the project was primarily about listening. With the help of professional consultants from The Learning Group, Inc., of Denver, Colorado, the school listened to hundreds of people—alums, students, faculty, staff, trustees, clergy, and laity in the wider community. The findings, analyzed and then translated into a marketing plan, are now being incorporated into the school's strategic planning process. I think it is safe to say that the plan has provided the basis for revitalized recruitment, educational program development, and fund raising efforts.

The market research included the following goals:

Assist Andover Newton in understanding the nature of the market (and submarkets) in which it operates.

Determine the awareness level of the school within its geographic area and its position within that market.

Ascertain the extent of need which exists for the school's present program offerings.

Identify possible new program offerings.

Determine donor attitudes and propensity for charitable contributions to the school.

Key research questions guided the thousands of surveys, interviews, and focus groups, held both on campus and off. A sampling of these questions follows:

What is the awareness level of the school in the regional marketplace?

What courses, programs, and services should the seminary offer in order to increase credit hours and enrollments?

When should the school schedule courses in order to increase credit hours and enrollments?

At what locations should the school offer its courses and programs?

What features should the school promote in order to increase enrollments and contributions?

The marketing study consisted primarily of internal and external assessments of the school and its markets. All design and interpretation of the survey materials, leadership of the focus groups, and coordination of research vehicles were conducted by professional marketing consultants.

The internal segment consisted of extensive interviews with staff, faculty, students (prospective, new, and continuing), alums, trustees, and donors, combined with survey questionnaires administered to some of these same groups. In addition, the researchers reviewed existing institutional and student recruitment literature and policies. Identification of institutional strengths and weaknesses helped focus our options for the future.

The external assessment consisted of survey questionnaires sent to alums, clergy, and lay members of the community. In addition, a competitive analysis of six other theological schools, identified to be in direct competition to Andover Newton, was conducted.

Partly as a result of the market research, the administration and board of trustees decided to develop a new strategic planning process, one that would take advantage of and incorporate the findings of the market research. Beginning with the mission statement—our ultimate guide through all the planning—we are now positioned to embrace the opportunities and challenges that await us during the 1990s and beyond.

Our experience with market research and planning helped us learn some important lessons:

Begin your research with a solid sense of the school's mission and identity. Let them be your anchor as you explore program options.

Watch out for language problems. Overuse of marketing terminology, buzz words, and concepts will alienate those most necessary for the plan's success—faculty, staff, alums, and the board! Use theological terms as a substitute whenever possible.

Be ready to devote sufficient staff time for the market research in support of your professional consultants. It will allow you to control the process rather than the other way around.

Be prepared to have your institutional assumptions challenged. Don't get defensive when you learn that your school is not meeting the needs of your constituency or that your school is perceived as ineffective in one or more areas.

Understand that market research is not a one-time exercise but ongoing. Once you begin to plan and develop programs on the basis of "market realities," future choices for program development will be most effective if based on continuing research and analysis.

Be prepared to think in terms of what is best for "the customer"—our students, churches, and alums—as opposed to what is most comfortable or easiest for the school.

Shaping Theological Education in a Cyberspace Society

Thomas K. Craine

Bill Easum gave a lecture at Iliff recently, and opened his remarks with a great cartoon. Imagine a contented cow, perhaps the Borden mascot, with a halo around its head. The caption: Sacred cows make great hamburger.

Easum is a consultant, a futurist, and a commentator on the current condition of the mainline church and its prospects. Seeing those prospects as bleak is an optimistic position for him. Without dramatic change, requiring major paradigm shifts, he believes our churches are on the same course as the dinosaurs—and by implication so are our seminaries.

Because I'll be advancing ideas that may give those with sacred cows indigestion, let me briefly share some personal background. First, I'm a lay person. Second, while I am relatively new to theological education, I've been in higher education nearly thirty years and understand that culture very well. Third, I grew up and continue to be active in the church, and think I know local church culture well also. I care deeply about both higher education and the church. Those two institutions are the primary protectors of our culture and transmitters of our values. Both are in serious trouble today. They are in trouble in large measure because they are businesses and they fail to perceive that reality. More on that later.

My objectives are to:

take a look at change—the cyberspace society in which we now operate;

identify a few myths and old models that inhibit our fund raising ability in a rapidly changing world;

present a new paradigm for development officers as shapers of theological education;

suggest ways for us to move into and operate within this new paradigm.

What is a paradigm? In his book, *Future Edge,* Joel Barker defines a paradigm as "a set of rules and regulations (written and unwritten) that does two things: 1) it establishes or defines boundaries; and 2) it tells you how to behave inside those boundaries in order to be successful."

Let me begin by sharing two progressions and one equation. The first progression is: 2, 6, 18, 54, _? The answer, of course, is 162. The second progression is: IBM, GM, AE, EK, HE, _? The answer this time is not so easy. IBM of course is "big blue," GM represents General Motors, AE is American Express, EK is Eastman Kodak, and HE is higher education. The answer is TE, theological education.

What did all the corporations in the second progression have in common? Basically, they became complacent. They were content with who they were and what they did. GM didn't seem to care if you wanted what it produced—large, gas-guzzling vehicles. That is what people had always purchased. Those were the only product lines. GM had the majority of market share, and who would want to buy those tiny made-in-Japan cars anyway? Similarly, IBM was prepared to have you purchase any computer you wanted. It didn't matter, it made nearly all of them. And then, in a garage of all places, two guys started making Apple computers, and forced IBM to change dramatically. American Express, Eastman Kodak, and numerous others underwent similar experiences. All of these companies failed to stay abreast of changing markets, technological advances, and to be concerned with customer needs. All of these companies experienced major paradigm shifts.

Higher education, theological education, and the church are now experiencing similar paradigm shifts. Many who work in these sectors, however, are having a difficult time recognizing this reality, much less strategizing on how to deal successfully with it.

That leads to a single equation: HE + church = ? The

answer is a seminary. The *combination* of the institutions of higher education and the church yields a seminary. Neither of these institutions is recognized for its ability to respond quickly to change, make difficult choices, and shape its own future. Their cultures, values, and decision processes mitigate against it. We face a new millennium in which the speed of change will make the present look like slow motion. With paradigms shifting rapidly, our future can be seen all too clearly in the past of our corporate brethren.

How will the following paradigm shifts affect us in 1995 and beyond?

churches that are increasingly run by laity,

denominational identification becoming less important to laity,

the discovery by laity that the church isn't relevant,

seminaries not being seen as relevant—at least to the corporate world,

an increasing decline in the number of our traditional supporters,

recognizing we are a business.

Interestingly, the Association of Theological Schools (ATS) is a paradigm within which those who work in seminaries live. It establishes rules and defines success within those rules. Currently ATS is attempting to shift paradigms as it reconsiders its accreditation standards in an effort to more nearly define "the good theological school." Whether that paradigm shift will be dramatic enough to accommodate the cyberchange we face remains to be seen.

Let me suggest that we in development, along with our institutions, continue to operate out of a few old myths and paradigms. *Our failure to change keeps us trapped in the donation business rather than the investment business.*

Certain of these old myths are identified by Don Joiner in his book, *Christians and Money.* Here's one: wealth is sinful. That myth implies if people are wealthy, they must have done (or are doing) something illegal or immoral. Joiner hears this frequently from many churches in many ways. If he hears it, so do our donors. This message not only conflicts with their understanding of money, it also appears hypocritical to them. They hear they aren't supposed to have any money, yet we keep asking them for more of it. As a donor you might get the impression that our real mission is to redistribute wealth from the rich to the poor. That persistent message erroneously suggests that wealth is finite, that there is only a certain amount of money to go around, and the name of the game is to reallocate it. That makes no sense to our donors. It confirms for them that we simply do not understand how money and wealth are generated—through human creativity. And to put that into a theological context for a moment, remember we are created in the Creator's image.

Further, there is the subtle and persistent suggestion in our environment that money is the root of all evil. As Joiner points out, that is probably the greatest misunderstanding about money we will ever hear. It is not money per se, but the love of money in which evil often becomes rooted. Yet many people in our business—faculty, administration, and alums—are remarkably uncomfortable with money. For whatever reasons, many who work in the church and seminary sense money talk is "grubby" talk, not church-like, not God talk. They are even more uncomfortable with our economic system, which generates the resources we seek. They often appear to treat that system like an embarrassing family relative with whom they have to live, but they sure don't like it.

Another paradigm is reported by the Murdock Charitable Trust in a recent study of graduate theological education:

*Within the present paradigm professors—
the faculty—have control of their courses,
their classes, the curriculum, and faculty
hiring and tenure decisions. This existing
structure is reinforced by tradition, the
accrediting associations and government
structures. It cannot be changed by trustees,
denominations, administrators or donors.*

221

> *Yet in many cases what's needed is a realization*
> *by seminary boards, administration, and faculty*
> *that they will not survive if they continue to look*
> *to past successes and old paths rather than deal*
> *realistically with the changes needed to assure*
> *their graduates will give leadership to the*
> *churches of the next century.*

Yet another paradigm suggests we are not a business and that business principles do not apply to us. This paradigm considers business words such as customer, accountability, markets, products, niche, competitive advantage, strategies, priorities, and leveraging to border on profanity. The concepts of re-engineering and TQM (total quality management) are dismissed as not being especially applicable to our industry. Indeed, when ATS began its reaccreditation standards project (paradigm shift), it pointed out in orientation sessions that this was not a TQM effort.

One final old paradigm says that we are relevant. We learned from our ATS case study two years ago that surely was not true from the corporate community's perspective. I suspect it is increasingly untrue for our major constituents as well.

The world in which we now operate is approaching quantum speed, yet the institutions we represent continue in many respects to operate in 19th century ways. We follow paradigms that worked well in the past, but will not provide the rules we need for the future. Our success in securing resources for our schools is intimately tied to that reality.

There are many axioms in fund raising. A few of my favorites are:

It takes money to make money;

The right person has to ask the right prospect for the right amount for the right thing at the right time;

The competition is for leadership, not for money;

Eventually somebody has to ask somebody for some money!

Let me share one more that I have come to believe is fundamental to all we do. As much as I have heard it, it is only recently that I began to hear it with new ears:

People won't invest in operating budgets; they donate. They invest in the vision and the programs and the solutions that operating budgets make possible.

This leads me to suggest a new paradigm: Development programs in the future will do more than simply generate resources for the institution of which they are a part. *They will serve as catalysts for basic institutional change.* They will do this by becoming advocates for, and involved in, thoughtful, disciplined, institutional strategic planning.

Strategic planning is all about change; about translating institutional vision into reality; about narrowing the disparity between what we say and what we do; about moving our institutions from the business of donation to that of investment.

Informed, realistic planning can make an important difference to an institution's future. It establishes clear priorities, shapes budget allocations, and guides everyday institutional behavior. Typically, the planning in which we have engaged has consisted of collecting dreams and wishes, binding them together in an attractive document, and then placing it on the shelf. Usually this has been adequate to satisfy both ATS's requirements for institutional planning and a comprehensive campaign's need for a case statement.

Thoughtful, disciplined institutional planning:

creates a common context for decision making by establishing operating assumptions regarding external and internal environments (e.g. economic, political, demographic, technical, and social forces; human, financial, and physical resources; institutional values and cultures; strengths and opportunities; and weaknesses and vulnerabilities);

implies establishing priorities and making choices;

establishes criteria for making judgments, such as quality, need (centrality, market, et cetera), and efficiency;

provides a guide to institutional action and is not adjunct to day-to-day operations;

is a continuous process, involving decision making

regarding evaluation and resource allocation;

integrates strategic plans with budget processes so that institutional and program specific priorities are reflected in the budget;

improves accountability;

enables the core responsibilities of trusteeship, leadership, and stewardship to be fulfilled.

With ATS's assistance, we have begun to compare our performance with two distinct peer groups. It is an enlightening exercise to see how we compare with our peers on, for example, our institution's percentage of expenditures by area or our gift income totals and support per FTE student.

What does all this have to do with our roles as development officers? It allows us to help our institutions move from the business of donations to that of investment. Isn't that what our business should be? The opportunity to be in that business, to shape the future of society by helping to shape our schools through strategic planning, is a vision and calling I can truly get excited about.

Clearly I am suggesting a major paradigm shift in how we see our roles and responsibilities—and *how others see them.*

I am encouraging all in seminary development to roll up their sleeves and take on the role of institutional change agent. I am absolutely convinced that we not only can, but need to do it. In fact we are uniquely positioned for this new role.

Our advantage is that change comes from those outside, in the margin, on the fringe, and that is where most of us in our institutions operate—without faculty appointment, tenure, or academic portfolios. We are the linchpin between seminary and society and we interact more with church and lay constituencies, with corporations, with people in the for-profit world—with our customers—than about anyone else in our schools. We experience and live in change daily. We have a unique window on the world out there to bring to the table. More importantly, we are less vested in what is and more vested in what can be. That is the nature of our jobs, of helping to both create and fulfill vision.

Strategic planning, at the institutional level, is the foundation of our work. It empowers serious fund raising. Our success depends upon it.

What can we do? I contend a tremendous amount. Here are some suggestions:

Identify soul mates inside and outside our institutions.

Establish communication systems and newsletters.

Access and report on peer comparisons/databases.

Share futures information/ reports.

Be aware of what the competition is doing.

Work with board members.

Affirm trustee responsibilities to ensure planning occurs.

Establish clear institutional priorities for fund raising.

Be an advocate for institutional authenticity.

Prepare and circulate planning papers, citing the need for and value of planning.

Work for a quality improvement environment.

Initiate customer audits.

Obtain donor feedback.

Help create futuring committees.

Clarify where responsibility for strategic planning lies.

Bring business language and paradigms into your institution.

Prepare a strategic plan for your own office.

Seek grants to secure external funding for institutional strategic planning initiatives.

Relate strategic planning to increased support.

I have suggested that the rules, the old paradigms within which our institutions function, are changing dramatically; that we in development are uniquely positioned to create a new paradigm for ourselves and our institutions; that we can bring transforming energy to our institutions through strategic planning to help shape theological education in this new, cyberspace society; by moving into this new paradigm we can move our institutions out of the donation business and into the investment business.

The Decentralization
of Theological Education

Lyn C. Perez

The growth of technology has brought innumerable changes to our world. Our kitchens now have microwaves, changing the way we cook and the way we eat. Our telephones are portable, so we can reach out and touch someone while in downtown traffic or on the golf course. Our cars talk to us, we no longer do arithmetic in our heads, the movies have come to our living rooms, and we check our computers instead of our mailboxes for mail. The list goes on and on.

However, the most significant result of the growth of technology is that it has made our world much smaller. It has turned the globe into a global village. Travel to Europe is no more time consuming now than a trip to another state in years past. A letter or a document can be in the hands of someone in Asia only minutes after being placed in a fax machine in Nebraska.

The advances in transportation and communication have connected the continents and have caused a decentralization of business and education throughout the world. Because of these advances, we now have an opportunity to teach laity and bring theological education to the church in ways which, until recently, would not have been possible. Through technology we have the opportunity to increase our effectiveness and serve a wider portion of the church. We can do so through more cost effective means.

Whether one is called to the pastorate or is a lay person wishing to engage in serious theological study, it is difficult to leave employment, sell a home, uproot the family, and move to another city to attend seminary. Students who do relocate to attend seminary usually find it necessary to obtain some type of employment, but most frequently do so at a much lower salary level than before. The support of churches, family, and friends is helpful, but it is often inadequate to cover all expenses. Student spouses often seek work, but they, too, receive wages at lower levels. For the seminarians who are married and have children, work is either not possible, or child care expenses absorb a large part of employment income.

Because most seminarians need the financial support of employment in order to attend seminary, it is necessary for us to consider how we can better provide a course of study for a working student's schedule. One way is changing the way classes are scheduled. At Reformed Theological Seminary, we now schedule courses in the evenings, on weekends, and in block fashion: three or four consecutive hours once a week rather than one hour a day on three separate days. We are challenging our faculty to think through other ways we might make theological education more accessible, even taking theological education to students rather than requiring them to come to us. Through technology we are able to provide educational opportunities in ways never before possible.

One way Reformed Theological Seminary has attempted to meet the challenge and bring theological education to the student is by opening new campuses in the larger metropolitan areas of Orlando, Florida, and Charlotte, North Carolina, where eight million people are within commuting distance to each campus and where there is a significant presence of constituent churches. This strategy has worked well, evidenced by an enrollment of more than nine hundred new students at these two campuses in just a few short years. We have also provided extension classes in numerous other locations throughout Mississippi, Florida, North Carolina, Virginia, Maryland, and California.

Additionally, we have aggressively developed an External Education program using audio tape lectures. Our External Education program has proved itself a cost effective delivery system for theological education. It maximizes the contribution of the very best teachers without excessive and tiring travel to remote locations. It also permits theological education to become as accessible and convenient as possible.

We recognize that while traditional resident campuses will still be needed and have their own value and appeal, it is apparent that education is in the incipient stages of a transformation that will result in new delivery systems making theological education more cost effective, more accessible, and more convenient.

Many universities and colleges have discovered the benefits of—and are utilizing—satellite transmission, cable television, and videoconferencing to offer courses. Courses offered in this manner offer a flexibility similar to an audio tape course, yet combine the strengths of residence courses by providing spontaneity, real time interaction, and a visual component to the learning experience.

Courses offered through these means make sense for theological education as well. With a satellite dish, a large screen television, and a speakerphone, a church could offer a full seminary training program without members diminishing their active participation in the life of the church. This could be done at a significantly lower cost to both the student and to the church than traditional education. A student could maintain employment and continue involvement in the church, causing minimal disruption to family life. Students could also remain under the guidance and nurture of the pastor and church during this ministerial education, permitting them to provide support to the students' pastoral development in a way unlikely to take place at a distance.

Another important consideration in evaluating the use of this technology is cost. The cost of transmitting courses by satellite or through a fiber optic network is relatively fixed, while at the same time it provides the opportunity to reach virtually an unlimited number of students. Unlike residence campuses, where costs for faculty and facilities actually rise with increasing enrollments, the unit cost of providing a theological education by satellite to a student will continually decrease as enrollment increases.

One of the most pressing needs of our era is training for

laity. While much has been said and written about equipping the laity, churches during this century have become more and more dependent upon leadership from the clergy. Spiritually-robust churches require strong lay leadership, which will not emerge without learning and serving.

In recent years there has been a rising level of interest among laity for substantial biblical and theological education that would equip persons to understand and respond discerningly to cultural and religious issues and controversies. Such training strengthens churches and permits beneficial instruction and influence in the community.

Most lay persons do not have the luxury of leaving their jobs and attending seminary for one to three years. The quality of education provided to them by the local church, however, fails to match their needs and desires. This can be remedied by distance learning theological training programs.

Although there are positive economic and practical reasons to utilize technology for providing theological education, it is extremely important for the future health of the church that due care be given to the extent to which this technology is integrated into a program to train future pastors. A new generation of students with unique characteristics is being raised.

Theological educators must analyze and consider these characteristics when training this new generation as future ministers.

Pastoral education, in distinction to secular post-secondary education, is concerned not only with the level of content a student has mastered, but also the spiritual maturity and the level of practical skills the student has developed. The mistake most theological institutions make in addressing the application of new technology to pastoral education is either concluding that it is not possible at all without losing the essence of ministerial training or that a curriculum is automatically transferable using technology.

The "knowing" component of theological education—the cognitive, objective content of a subject—can easily be provided by satellite transmission. The "doing" component—preaching, pastoral counseling, leadership, evangelism, and Christian education training—will require a partnership with the church to oversee skill acquisition and development by providing labs, simulations, role playing, field work, and other practical experiences.

The mistake seminaries made in the past was to assume pastoral students could acquire practical skills after seminary while working in the church. In the last decade, Reformed Theological Seminary and other like-minded institutions have worked hard to develop curricula to assist in spiritual development and in skill acquisition. This part of the training is not automatically transferable by technology.

An educational program provided by both the seminary and the local church ultimately could be more effective than either might provide alone. The result could be increased effectiveness—well beyond what has yet been achieved—in training pastors.

Wal-Mart changed the face of retail sales forever through a new method of product distribution. Today, technology provides a means to change the way theological education is distributed to those in the church. It is only a matter of time before the face of the seminary is changed. As the saying goes, we will all have to "lead, follow, or get out of the way."

The New Face of Development

R. Mark Dillon

What changes can we expect in the development field? I lift up for your consideration ten potential changes:

First, our institutions will depend upon us more for viability. A remarkable transformation is taking place in the third sector, and educational development has led the way. As enrollment growth slows, and in some sectors disappears, as endowment income adjusts dramatically downward from the heady returns of the eighties to the austere realities of the nineties, as deferred maintenance bills pile up and operating expenses grow, presidents and trustees are looking to development to preserve the margin of excellence. I've told a number of new development staffers, "If you want job security, be an excellent development professional." There are lots of development people out there, but the good ones will command salary and respect, both within and outside the university.

Second, institutional loyalty will shrink as consumer demands grow. We've already seen that the boomers entering their peak earning years place less trust in institutions and are more directive in their giving. *The Chronicle of Philanthropy* reports that the United Way, from 1989-1991, has seen the amount of contributions earmarked for specific causes or charities increase by forty-two percent. We dare not take loyalty, either from alums or long-term donors and friends, for granted. We must also provide a variety of gift opportunities within the institutional mission to meet the varied interests of our donors.

Third, competition will become more fierce. Our success will be challenged from two directions. The top schools are getting more sophisticated in institutional development. It used to be that we could let the very large organizations stake their territory and count on the unsophisticated segment of the third-sector organizations to give us a foothold. As more organizations add development programs and recruit top development people, we may find that our good development programs now look merely average. As more organizations upgrade their programs (for every nonprofit that goes out of business, three are born), there will be potential decline in our ability to attract major funding.

Fourth, planned giving will cease to be an auxiliary to development and will become the central thrust. *Fortune* magazine recently estimated that between 1990 and 2010, $8 trillion will change hands between the post-World War II generation and the baby boomer generation. It will be the largest transfer of wealth in the history of the United States.

If this is true, I offer two observations: First, I'm no economist, but that is one big pile of money, and we'd better be thinking about how we can get our institution's share of that transfer of wealth. Second, I don't know about you, but I trust the charitable instincts of my parents' generation more than I do those of my own generation.

If you buy those two observations, we are in a window of opportunity where planned gifts can meet the current needs of these potential donors, provide for their children appropriately, and meet their philanthropic goals—and ours. It used to be that one planned giving officer in a development office was a luxury. Now, every development professional will need to have an understanding of the basic planned giving instruments and the mindset that every donor is a prospect for a major planned gift.

Fifth, faculties will not only tolerate our presence; they will call us colleagues, and some even friends. Now, I grant you, this may be looking way into the future. Trachtman said it well when he observed, "To most faculty members I know, the world of university advancement is *terra incognita.* They think of the advancement officer vaguely—if at all—as a salesperson and petitioner who haunts corporate and foundation board rooms and is likely, in Emily Dickinson's sly language, to 'tell all the truth, but tell it slant.'"

However, as our professionalism increases, as the fruits

of our labor, out of necessity, contribute more to the well-being of the university, and as philanthropy emerges as a legitimate subject of academic inquiry, we may indeed gain the respect and even the appreciation of our esteemed faculty colleagues.

Sixth, the study of philanthropy will emerge from a novel subject to a serious academic concern. When in the mid-eighties I began to search for graduate programs that would give theoretical substance to my career in development, I found exactly two: the MSA (Master of Science in Administration) program in Non-Profit Management at Notre Dame University, and the Philanthropy and Leadership program at the Union Institute under the leadership of James Fisher, president emeritus of CASE. The Center on Philanthropy, to the best of my knowledge, was at that time only in the dream stage.

Today there are programs, primarily at the master's level, in philanthropy, volunteerism, and nonprofit management at, to name but a few, Boston College, Case Western Reserve University, City University of New York, Duke University, Indiana University, Johns Hopkins University, New School for Social Research, Northwestern University, Seton Hall University, Texas Christian University, Tufts University, University of California-San Francisco, University of Minnesota, and University of Pennsylvania.

Just recently the International Society for Third-Sector Research was established. Dedicated to promoting research and teaching, the society will be based at the Institute for Policy Studies of the Johns Hopkins University. The academy is coming to appreciate the discipline of philanthropic study and to embrace the study of the third sector as a legitimate academic concern.

Seventh, philanthropy will cross national boundaries. While American philanthropy is significant and in some regards unique, voluntary action for the public good is an international phenomenon.

A recent issue of *The Chronicle of Philanthropy* reports that a new group aimed at promoting the development of philanthropy worldwide has been started by representatives of nineteen countries. The group, says the *Chronicle,* "an association of donors and charities, hopes to compile and exchange information about non-profit activities around the world and promote citizens' involvement in their societies. The group is expected to adopt the name CIVICUS: World Alliance for Citizen Participation. It will share offices with Independent Sector, a Washington-based coalition of grant-makers and charities." Philanthropy will cross national boundaries.

The largest cash gift my school has ever received was given last year. It was given by the president of a large business. Not so unusual, except this person was a Korean business woman who has never lived in the United States. The new development officer must think globally or miss out on magnificent possibilities.

Eighth, women will break the glass ceiling in development. The *Wall Street Journal* reported that the percentage of women in the development field has shown a marked increase in the past ten years. Sixty-nine percent of employees in the independent sector are female, compared to forty-six percent for all employees in the United States. Women account for fifty-four percent of CASE's membership and fifty-eight percent within NSFRE.

Unfortunately, women have a way to go to achieve equality in our profession, but I believe it will come. Twelve years ago, when I entered the field, I attended a fund raising conference in which the male presenter said it would be inappropriate for a woman to ask a prospective donor, male or female, for a gift. Apparently these attitudes are sometimes reflected in salary scales. NSFRE reports that the woman's average salary in the development field is about $12,000 below that of her male counterparts.

However, more and more women are becoming the chief development officer at their institutions. The glass ceiling in our profession will be broken.

Ninth, development professionals, more and more, will come to lead in education and third-sector organizations. It used to be that college and university presidents came from the faculty ranks. More and more, colleges and universities are seeing that skills in conveying the mission and securing major gifts are essential duties of the president. They are calling upon development professionals who know education, of course, but who also can secure the major gift.

Just for fun I looked in *The Chronicle of Higher Education* for 1971 to look at ads for presidencies of colleges or universities. Very few even mentioned development skills as a requirement. Listings for Positions Wanted read as follows: "Experience as science chairman and academic dean. Developer of programs and faculties." Another one: "Published author, experienced department chairman, and academic dean, dedicated hard worker, seeks a 16-hour-a-day presidency." And yet another: "Academic and management experience for small, private college. Available July or September."

Any of us who leaf through the bulletin board of *The Chronicle* these days, usually after a discouraging week, will note that it is rare to see any presidential profile which does not highlight the requirement that the presidential candidate have ability and experience in raising major gifts. The future will see many more college and university presidents come from the development ranks.

Tenth, the impulse to give cannot be assumed; it must be taught and awakened. When I make fund raising calls today, it is usually to people well over fifty. I can almost always make the assumption that 1) they feel grateful and fortunate to have acquired what they have, 2) they have a desire and even a need to give something back, 3) that desire is almost always rooted in a religious background and sense of stewardship, and 4) they have a high view of education.

I'm not nearly as certain that the forty-year-old who made $400,000 last year feels the same way. That doesn't mean he or she is more selfish than the older generation. I'm just not certain that the values of the parents have made their way clearly into his or her culture. If that is true, it will call for more patience, more research, more teaching, and more cultivation than we've ever had to produce in the past.

Currents of change will continue to swirl in society, in education, and in the profession of fund development. They always have, they always will. Our choices are to be swept up by the changes, to stand resolutely against the winds of change, or to anticipate and lead.

Those who are swept up and even surprised by change will inevitably be passed by. Those who resolutely turn their backs to the winds of change will become the sad, pathetic underclass of our profession who live off philanthropy rather than for philanthropy.

Those who anticipate the changes and lead the way will define the profession of development, will help preserve the greatness and distinctiveness of the educational enterprise, and will chart a new and even better course of voluntary action for the public good.

The future of our profession is largely in our hands. We must choose to anticipate, to contribute effectively to a cause far greater than mere existence, to challenge the human spirit to fulfill its purpose—in short, to make a difference.

We, as development professionals, are uniquely poised to shape the future of our profession, of the educational enterprise, and through it, society. That, in my view, is a life worth living and a vocation worth pursuing.

If I can call you back to the "Field of Dreams," you will remember that as Shoeless Joe and the young Archie Graham analyzed the situation and projected into the future, they determined that Knuckles would throw one low and outside. That's what the pitcher threw, and Archie hit an RBI.

I've tried to analyze our situation and make some guesses about what may be coming next. With a bit of luck— and perhaps divine providence—we may be in for the exhilaration of the professional equivalent of an RBI.

About the Authors

Bill L. Barnes is retired and living in Scottsdale, Arizona. He was previously vice president for development at Christian Theological Seminary in Indianapolis, Indiana.

Harold R. Blatt is semi-retired and living in Collegeville, Pennsylvania. He was previously vice president for institutional advancement at Eastern Baptist Theological Seminary in Philadelphia, Pennsylvania.

Wesley F. Brown is associate dean at Duke University Divinity School in Durham, North Carolina.

Ray M. Caraway is associate director of The United Methodist Foundation of Louisiana. He was previously director of development at Garrett-Evangelical Theological Seminary in Evanston, Illinois.

Fred W. Cassell is vice president for seminary relations at Princeton Theological Seminary in Princeton, New Jersey.

Kim E. Clark is director of charitable estate and gift planning at Pacific School of Religion in Berkeley, California.

Daniel Conway is secretary for planning, communications, and development for the archdiocese of Indianapolis. He was previously vice president for planning and development at Saint Meinrad Seminary in Saint Meinrad, Indiana.

Donald R. Cooney is director of planned giving at Gettysburg College in Gettysburg, Pennsylvania. He was previously vice president for development at Lancaster Theological Seminary in Lancaster, Pennsylvania.

Thomas K. Craine is vice president for institutional advancement at Iliff School of Theology in Denver, Colorado.

William R. Cunitz is vice president for advancement and enrollment management at Andover Newton Theological School in Newton Centre, Massachusetts.

R. Mark Dillon is vice president for advancement at Wheaton College in Wheaton, Illinois. He was previously senior vice president of institutional advancement at Trinity Evangelical Divinity School in Deerfield, Illinois.

Jewell Perkins Eanes is director of seminary relations at Garrett-Evangelical Theological Seminary in Evanston, Illinois.

Richard Eppinga is assistant to the president for advancement at Calvin Theological Seminary in Grand Rapids, Michigan.

Alicia McNary Forsey is dean of continuing education and stewardship at Starr King School for the Ministry in Berkeley, California.

Royal A. Govain is a development consultant and English teacher in Paraiba, Brazil. He was previously associate dean for development at Harvard Divinity School in Cambridge, Massachusetts.

F. Stuart Gulley is president of LaGrange College in LaGrange, Georgia. He was previously associate vice president for university development and church relations at Emory University in Atlanta, Georgia.

David P. Harkins is vice president for development and administration at Eden Theological Seminary in St. Louis, Missouri.

David L. Heetland is editor of *Seminary Development News* and vice president for development at Garrett-Evangelical Theological Seminary in Evanston, Illinois.

Fred L. Hofheinz is program director, religion, for the Lilly Endowment, Inc., in Indianapolis, Indiana.

Mark A. Holman is a PhD candidate in higher education policy at the University of California at Berkeley. He was previously director of the annual fund and alum relations at Pacific Lutheran Theological Seminary in Berkeley, California.

Billie Hooker is vice president for Central State University in Wilberforce, Ohio. She was previously director of the office of institutional advancement at the Interdenominational Theological Center in Atlanta, Georgia

Chase S. Hunt is director of planned giving at Princeton Theological Seminary in Princeton, New Jersey.

Don R. Locher is special assistant to the president at the School of Theology at Claremont in Claremont, California.

Celia Luxmoore lives in Arlington, Virginia. She was previously director of development at Vancouver School of Theology in Vancouver, British Columbia.

David Mertz is associate director of development at Rutgers University in New Brunswick, New Jersey. He was previously associate director of development for theological and graduate schools at Drew University in Madison, New Jersey.

Frank A. Mullen is director of development at Yale University Divinity School in New Haven, Conneticut.

Michaeline O'Dwyer, RSHM, is vice president for development and public relations at the Jesuit School of Theology at Berkeley in Berkeley, California.

Donovan J. Palmquist is retired and living in Chicago, Illinois. He was previously vice president for development at the Lutheran School of Theology at Chicago.

Lynwood C. Perez is vice president for development at Reformed Theological Seminary in Orlando, Florida.

John J. M. O'Brien-Prager is director of professional studies and immigration liaison at Princeton Theological Seminary in Princeton, New Jersey. He was previously director of annual giving at the school.

Paul C. Reinert, SJ, is chancellor emeritus of Saint Louis University in Saint Louis, Missouri.

Anita M. Rook is a realtor with Carpenter Realtors in Indianapolis, Indiana. She was previously vice president for development at Christian Theological Seminary in Indianapolis, Indiana.

Delora A. Roop is receptionist and office coordinator of institutional advancement at Bethany Theological Seminary in Richmond, Indiana.

Daniel A. Schipp is vice president for development at Saint Meinrad School of Theology in Saint Meinrad, Indiana.

Douglas H. Scott is associate vice president/director of planned and major gifts for Walker Methodist Foundation in Minneapolis, Minnesota. He was previously vice president for development at Central Baptist Theological Seminary in Kansas City, Kansas.

Bruce C. Stewart is president and professor emeritus at Reformed Presbyterian Theological Seminary in Pittsburgh, Pennsylvania.

Martin P. Trimble is lead organizer for the Wilmington Interfaith Network in Wilmington, Delaware. He was previously a program officer for religion at The Pew Charitable Trusts.

Cheryl Tupper is director for the faculty grants resource center at The Association of Theological Schools in Pittsburgh, Pennsylvania.

Larry D. VanDyke is president of CMA - Resource Development, Inc. in Johnson City, Tennessee. He was previously executive director of development at Emmanuel School of Religion in Johnson City, Tennessee.

M. Katherine Welles-Snyder is director of institutional advancement at Hartford Seminary in Hartford, Conneticut.

James M. Wray, Jr. is vice president for development at Lexington Theological Seminary in Lexington, Kentucky.

John W. Zehring is senior pastor of South Parish Congregational Church in Augusta, Maine. He was the founding editor of *Seminary Development News* and was previously vice president for development at Bangor Theological Seminary in Bangor, Maine.